THE LAW OF THELEMA
HIDDEN ALCHEMY

THE LAW
OF
THELEMA
HIDDEN ALCHEMY

Oliver St. John

The Law of Thelema—Hidden Alchemy

© Oliver St. John 2024

All Rights Reserved. No part of this publication may be reproduced, distributed, or transmitted in any form or by any means, including photocopying, recording, or other electronic or mechanical methods, without the prior written permission of the author, except in the case of brief quotations embodied in critical reviews and certain other non-commercial uses permitted by copyright law.

© Cover art, design and graphics Oliver St. John 2024

ISBN 978-1-7391549-4-3

ORDO ASTRI IMPRIMATUR

www.ordoastri.org

But remember, o chosen one, to be me; to follow the love of Nu in the star-lit heaven; to look forth upon men, to tell them this glad word.

Contents

Preface	i
Stele of Revealing (obverse; photograph)	—
The Star of Revealing	1
Love under Will	4
The Hermetic Great Work	10
The Beast and Leviathan	17
The Sphinx: Symbol of Love and Will	23
The Sphinx: Time and Alchemy	28
The Sphinx: Cycle of Ascent and Descent (diagram)	30
The Holy Guardian Angel	38
The Last Judgement	45
Initiation of the Ka—The Alchemical Secret	55
Stele of Revealing (reverse; photograph)	—
Appendices	—
Restoration of the Sphinx	65
Sphinx: Chronological Table	66
Tree of Life: Principal Correspondences	68
Hermetic Tree of Life (illustration)	69
Microcosmos and Egyptian Parts of the Soul	70
Tree of Life and the Four Worlds	71
Glossary	73
Selected Works of Oliver St. John	—

Preface

Sophia is our Guiding Light.

At the end of an entire Manvantara or 'world', mankind stands upon the threshold of total dissolution. Even those with a spiritual orientation, or what passes for that now, have not resisted the temptation of seeking a return to Eden through the use and adaptation of traditional sciences without comprehension, owing to ignorant rejection of all traditional (and so *principial*) knowledge. This folly has resulted in the awakening of very dangerous atavisms, of the Qliphotic order, and that are impossible to control by profane persons lacking highly specialised knowledge. Likewise, the System of Antichrist, to accomplish its plan of turning humans into robots or machines, has created countless forms of counterfeit initiation and spirituality that lack any true principle. Such forms bear a likeness or resemblance to the doctrines from which they were plundered, but they recognise no divine authority, replacing God with man, to whom 'wellbeing' is a primary concern in a time where irrationality and madness in all its forms prevail. Likewise, the apostles of Antichrist who, in all sincerity, wish to 'save the planet' are only echoing their own fatal preoccupation with the body and materiality above all else. Most are content to place their faith in conventional science at no matter what cost. They sleep in the deep trance of media technology, deluded into thinking that pressing a virtual button that seems to do everything for them gives them power. These are unknowing and unconcerned, blindly carrying out 'business as usual' such as trading, property acquisition and procreation. Initiates must seek the Way of Return, and that means not being susceptible to any of these traps.

The aim of this present work, our final word on Thelema, and which is an updated and corrected edition of several previous books, is to establish what is called the Law of Thelema in the context of the Hermetic tradition from whence it has its origins. Hermeticism may be accurately construed as 'that which came out of Egypt', after the decline of its language and civilisation. It must be clearly understood that the present work owes nothing at all to the thinking of Aleister Crowley or of his followers. Our purpose is to reveal the secrets of alchemy and the transfiguration of the soul that are encrypted in the text of Liber AL. Thus we may find a way out of the snares of modern and postmodern occultism and free our minds from the mantras that orchestrate the 'dance of the lemmings' into the Abyss.

The mainstream notion of the (Egyptian) Book of the Law, Liber AL vel Legis, is filtered through the obfuscating lens of the mind of the self-styled 'Beast', Crowley, which was steeped in the modern Western philosophy of Leibnitz, the New Science of the time and of course the ever-popular neo-spiritualism or occultism. Some of the fanatical followers of the cults of Thelema, having no clear idea of how to interpret the Book of the Law, and that are not in any way well learned in source works or in traditional knowledge, take the writings of Crowley, however far-fetched, as Gospel. They attach a mysterious value to the Book of the Law as a 'holy relic', which amounts to the worst kind of superstition. Most of these are beyond helping but there will always be those who have unhappily strayed into the nets and snares of neo-spiritualist Thelema and, retaining perhaps a genuine 'sense of eternity', still seek truth and real knowledge. For these, seeking truth requires first finding a way out of the trap they have fallen into. It is those that we primarily wrote this book for, even in its earliest forms.[1] There are others, however, who will find that this work reveals something never before disclosed concerning the hidden, alchemical nature of Thelema.

We should mention here for the benefit of our readership that the principle of soul and body is referred to throughout this present volume as feminine, while the principle of spirit and mind is treated as masculine. This is a literary and even a metaphysical convention in the languages of more than one spiritual tradition that was continued in the Book of the Law, which is of course the subject of this writing.

Much of the language and symbolism of the Book of the Law has its origin in the Egyptian and Judaeo Christian tradition. The latter was well known to Crowley, especially in the Protestant form that he grew up with and wished to rebel against. He likewise only knew the Egyptian tradition superficially, through the syncretism of the Order of the Golden Dawn, of which he was a member for a short time before the well-documented schism that ended it. For example, the symbols of the Beast and the Scarlet Woman can be traced to the Revelation or Apocalypse of St. John, the last book of the Christian New Testament. The doctrine that is typified in Christianity by the assumption of the Virgin Mary predates the Christian era, and is portrayed in the Book of the Law as the Scarlet Woman or Soul.

---

[1] Previous works include *The Ending of the Words—Magical Philosophy of Aleister Crowley* and *The Law of Thelema—Quantum Yoga*.

The legend of the Christ or Saviour who passes through trial and ordeal to be born in spirit was well founded at the Egyptian cult centre Aunnu, known by the Greeks as Heliopolis and called On in the biblical Old Testament. Here was celebrated the birth, death and resurrection of the hawk-headed star-god, Horus. In the Book of the Law, this god takes various forms. Among these are the Sphinx, the Dwarf Soul, and the Angel of Judgement.[2] The Khabs, the Khu and the Ka are ancient Egyptian pictographic symbols, and the many gods mentioned in the book are specific to the transformative rôles played by deity (*neteru*, properly speaking) at cult centres of Egypt such as Thebes and Heliopolis.

The Book of the Law, later commonly known as Liber AL vel Legis or simply 'Liber AL' was, according to its writer Crowley (1875–1947), communicated to him from a praeterhuman intelligence via the mediumship of his wife, Rose.[3] It should be mentioned here that on the holograph MS of the book, Crowley scribbled a line or two—later crossed out—to say it was an example of 'automatic writing', which was a method used by spiritists. According to him, the book proclaimed the advent of the New Aeon of Horus. The book was dictated in Cairo, 1904 by a praeterhuman intelligence called Aiwass. Named as the 'minister of Hoor-paar-kraat' in the book, the work of Aiwass was to reveal the law governing a new phase of human spiritual 'evolution'. We say 'according to him', because we do not in any way accept that Crowley was some kind of avatar, and we do not for one moment accept that any 'New Aeon' commenced in 1904, which is sheer fantasy. In the present work we refer to the traditional Hindu doctrine of Cosmic Cycles whenever we need to examine the subject of time in relation to the changing forms that the primordial tradition uses to keep us informed as to the true state of affairs.

---

[2] Christ is often confused with Osiris. The confusion is common with neo-spiritualists, and Crowley was no exception. Whereas Osiris remains in the underworld as Lord of the Dead, Christ and Horus both ascend to heaven. Heaven and paradise (or Amentet) are two quite different worlds.

[3] Crowley numbered the manuscript 'Liber XXX', a reference to the Qabalistic value of the letter 'L' that was the original title of the book: Liber L vel Legis. The book is also known as Liber CCXX (220 verses) as well as by the 'corrected' number, XXXI. Crowley added an Aleph (A = 1) to the *lamed* (L = 30). It is perhaps curious that there exists so much confusion over the identity of a book deemed so important to some!

Although it is very plausible that the contact Aiwass, known to us, though not to Crowley, as Kha'em'uast, son of Rameses II, was able to communicate some, a small part of the Book of the Law at least, through the medium Rose Edith Kelly (Mrs Crowley at the time), Aiwass did not interpret or comment on the meaning of what he said.[4] The notion of a 'new law for humanity', as Crowley put it, is not mentioned in the book and is pure fiction. Evolutionism was at that time very popular with the Theosophists and neo-spiritualists, who wished to interpret all traditional and ancient knowledge in the terms of modern science. No mention of any such plan is given in the book but the notion suited the ambitions of Crowley, which included setting up a kind of New World Order before the Theosophists could beat him to it.[5]

To continue with Crowley's ideas concerning the import of the Book of the Law, though we do not intend to spend too much time on what he thought: before a New Aeon can be incarnated or fixed in time, the word or truth of the previous aeon must be broken down and assimilated. Only then may Horus achieve his full expression. The operation is directed by Ra Hoor Khuit, the active counterpart and twin of Hoor-paar-kraat, the god of Silence. Ra Hoor Khuit is a martial god of 'Force and Fire' that embodies and manifests the powers of Saturn, the Lord of Time, and Mars. Through the ages, spiritual events are rooted in time. Man's understanding of himself and the cosmos is anchored by historical events—whether these are understood as real or imagined. Crowley, who accepted evolutionism in all its forms, suggested there are three aeons: Isis, Osiris and Horus. The Aeon of Isis represents a prehistoric time of matriarchy, where hunting and gathering predominated. After some considerable time came the patriarchal Aeon of Osiris, in which agriculture and civilisation flourished. The Aeon of Horus is then to be understood as the child of these parents, indicating a stage where individuals must take responsibility for their own actions.[6] This left Thelema wide open for psychological interpretation and still further reductionism by the later followers of Crowley who continue his cults today—albeit in a strangely hybrid sort of fashion.

---

[4] There is more detail concerning the nature of the Cairo Working of 1904, as well as that of such supra-human contacts, real or imagined, in our book *Babalon Unveiled—Thelemic Monographs* (Revised 2023).
[5] All of this was disclosed by the 'Beast' himself in his own writings.
[6] A somewhat trite and moralistic notion at best.

The 'three great Aeons' theory does not in any way concur with the precession of the equinoxes, though Crowley, in a very confused manner, attempts to assert that it does in his *The Book of Thoth*. According to some occultists, the Aeon of Horus as insisted upon by Crowley was abortive and ended in 1948—a mere forty-four years after the reception of Liber AL vel Legis! An Aeon of Maat then superseded the Aeon of Horus.[7] The notion here is that the Egyptian goddess Maat is the perfection of the Great Work or Hermetic Arcanum on earth. No aeon in *time* can truly be called 'perfect' however, and this looks all the more absurd when we consider it in the light of the real knowledge of the Cosmic Cycles in Hinduism. As we near the end of time, there is a degradation in terms of the manifest universe, not an improvement as evolutionists would have it in the face of all evidence to the contrary. None of these invented notions have anything to do with traditional wisdom concerning the Cosmic Cycles, greater or lesser. According to the Hindu doctrines—of which Crowley and his epigones knew very little—we are now at the end of the Age of Kali Yuga, where darkness and ignorance prevails. The ending of this, the final phase in a series of *manvantaras* or greater cosmic cycles, marks the *mahapralaya* or 'great dissolution' where all is withdrawn back into the supreme principle. In an instant, a new series of great cycles commences but for the present species of humanity we are now very close to the end. Evolutionism is exclusively a product of industrial modernity. A flower comes to bloom then fades and withers—it does not 'improve'.[8]

Liber AL vel Legis is scattered through with riddles requiring the use of the Qabalah, or to be more precise, Gematria, to unravel. The general reader, though, should have little difficulty in following the lines of our thought here: In Hebrew, as with Arabic and Greek, the letters are numbers and the numbers are letters. Words then produce a number that represents the value of that word. Meaning is then obtained from the relationship of words having the same numerical value. For example, the word Thelema, 'Will', adds to 93 by Greek, as does Agape, 'Love'. The will and love can be said to have related meaning. The name of Aiwass, the intelligence supposed to have transmitted the Book of the Law, is equal to the number 93 if we use the spelling *Aiwaz*. Aiwass is then identified with 'Will', or more exactly, *dharma* or otherwise *ordinance* in priestly matters.

---

[7] A student and disciple of Aleister Crowley, Frater Achad (Stansfeld Jones), put forward the year 1948 as the beginning of an Aeon of Maat.
[8] See 'Cosmic Cycles', *Nu Hermetica—Initiation and Metaphysical Reality*.

There is included in the Appendices a full glossary of technical terms used in the Book of the Law and elsewhere, plus key historical references. The Restoration of the Sphinx and Chronological Table place historical facts alongside biblical and other narratives to help the reader understand their context with the great events that have shaped civilisations.

We should emphasise once more that our book is in no way a study of the thought or the occult practices of Aleister Crowley. The following chapters do not in any way reflect his ideas or activities. This 'Thelema' will not be found on the Internet or even in other books on the subject. We could think of it as a Thelema that 'might have been', as a spiritual interpretation of those verses of the Book of the Law that were clearly heard from Aiwass and not made subject to distortion. Of course, it will never be possible to separate that book from the mind and hand of the man that wrote it down and for that reason we have revised our previous books on the subject and placed what has stood up to the test of time here, as a final word on a subject we do not intend pursuing further.

Sophia be-with-us forever.

Oliver St. John
Sol in ♊ Luna in ♐ 2024
Penwith Peninsula, Cornwall

The Stele of Revealing (obverse)

The Star of Revealing

In the year 1904 while in Cairo, Egypt, Aleister and Rose Crowley unwittingly earthed the transmission named the Book of the Law, Liber AL vel Legis. The *Stele of Revealing* that inspired the latter reveals the Great Work of an ancient Egyptian high priest and scribe at the Temple of Thebes, 'the opener of the doors of heaven', Ankh-af-na-khonsu. He was an initiate, a *ma-kheru* or one whose 'word is perfect (or true)'. The book addresses him as prophet; the name Ankh-af-na-khonsu was adopted by all members of an initiatic cult of Mentu. The ancient Egyptian name for Thebes was Waset, 'the place of ordination'. This involved the foreseeing of astronomical and other changes as well as the forecasting of future events by what is now called astrology.[9] The Great Work of the initiatic cult was the transformation of the soul through knowledge of the spiritual principles governing the operation. Liber AL vel Legis may then be considered to be, in part at least, a posthumous activation of this knowledge in fragmentary form, though couched in such terms as to bewilder and mislead fools. For some, it is no less than an ancient Egyptian curse.

It is these latter unfortunates that form the cults of Antichrist, in so far as an anti-spiritual force can be called a 'cult'. The ideals of Crowley cannot be separated from the milieu of the times in which he lived, which was to lay the foundation for modernism and later, the postmodernism and neo-socialist political theories that govern the present times. Thus, while Crowley's self-invented cults, based on his personal identification with the 'beast' of St. John's Revelation, seem to those who are attracted to them to reflect a spirit of rebellion and egoistic self-assertion, the consequence, as is clearly seen today, is abject slavery. The Antichrist is not an individual or a group but is a completely impersonal, demonic force that is the sum total of the anti-spiritual in all forms. Thus in other works we refer to this as the System of Antichrist, as it is more like a machine than any kind of living being.[10] It is *sub-infra*, in so far as it is barely in the realms of manifestation—yet it is the dominant influence on all worldly affairs today. The irony of imagining rebellion where only conformity and subjection exists, naturally escapes the followers of Antichrist.

---

[9] It should be made clear there is only the most tenuous relation between ancient astrology and what is now called that in modern times.
[10] See *Nu Hermetica—Initiation and Metaphysical Reality* and *The Way of Knowledge in the Reign of Antichrist*.

It is possible, nonetheless, to take the ambiguous wording of the (Egyptian) Book of the Law and reinterpret it according to the wisdom of real spiritual traditions and knowledge. Seen in that light, the book conveys knowledge concerning the union of the soul with that which lies wholly beyond the limits of the human individuality. Such knowledge is the means of her final liberation from all worlds of manifestation and death. Herein are the mysteries of the soul, veiled as the 'Scarlet Woman', and of her transfiguration. The colour of the soul is that of blood and fire. Her nature is lunar and therefore elemental. In union with the solar fire of the transmitter of the will current called the 'Beast' she is able to attain Hadit—who conveys the knowledge of her True Will.[11] Through Thelema or *love under will* she is fully realised as a 'star' in the immortal body of Nuit's company of heaven.[12]

To attain Hadit—the magical manifester of Nuit—the soul must turn her power inwards. It is only by this inward turning, which must involve the preparatory study of scriptural and other sacred texts and concentration of the mind in yoga that man is afforded spiritual realisation. Conjoined with the Beast, the Scarlet Woman represents the self-polarisation of an Initiate. Her consciousness is directed towards a union of solar fire and lunar magnetism. The child of this union is born of Nuit and Hadit, who communicate through the Beast and the Scarlet Woman, the Prophet and Bride. The divine offspring is Ra Hoor Khuit, Horus or Ra-Mentu.

Initiation thus opens the eye of the soul to the possibilities of immortal life and beyond that, eternity, thus bringing new meaning and possibilities to the earth life, freeing the soul from all that which confines and enslaves her to sorrow and death. The book may then be seen to speak of a spiritual path resting on relationship: individual existence defining itself by contrast with another by which it can know itself. The book has summarised the path of devotion (Sanskrit *bhakti*) in seven words:[13]

---

[11] The True Will, properly understood, is cognate with the Sanskrit *dharma*. See 'The Hermetic Great Work'.
[12] The 'Beast' is a name by which Crowley had already self-identified with, previous to the reception of Liber AL. What is expressed here is the ideal, of the *yogin* and his Shakti, though it was not to be fulfilled as Crowley abandoned Rose in Cairo. Thus in I: 15 he is told: 'But ye are not so chosen.'
[13] I: 57.

Love is the law, love under will.

The three chapters of the book each reveal a level of initiation. From the point of view of magick, the book begins with chapter three, not one. Wisdom has to be followed back to her source. The work thus begins with Ra Hoor Khuit, the Solar-Hermetic Lucifer whose action upon the soul prepares her for initiation. His instructions concern works of sorcery aimed at overcoming all obstacles encountered on the path. For the soul, such preparations are war. They require intelligent use of all her resources in order to deal effectively with enemies that are driven by the blind forces of the material universe.

I invoke, I greet thy presence, O Ra-Hoor-Khuit!

The above verse, III: 37, is translated from the *Stele of Revealing*, in which the priest and scribe Ankh-af-na-khonsu makes offering to the god, Ra Hoor Khuit, also known as Mentu—a form that combines Ra and Set-Typhon.

The establishment of Ra Hoor Khuit at the heart or centre of the soul leads to her encounter with Hadit, the giver of life who speaks through chapter two of the book. The encounter confers the keys of knowledge of a life only known through the knowledge of death. Through her union with Hadit, the Serpent of Knowledge, the soul contracts; she withdraws from the volatility and bewilderment of all sensory perceptions to be stabilised or alchemically 'fixed' as a star in the body of Nuit.

Thus, the way is open for the soul to partake of the joys of Nuit, participating in her divine ecstasy and love. Chapter one, the voice of Nuit, reveals the secret means of enjoying without restriction the ultimate relationship of opposites: that of individual consciousness and the Infinite, Absolute, unlimited eternal bliss.[14]

---

[14] The technical terms used here such as Nuit, Hadit and Ra Hoor Khuit will be explained through the commentary. There is also a concise glossary of terms in the Appendices to help the student.

Love under Will

To be initiated into the mysteries of Thelema, when this is interpreted from a spiritual point of view, is to be initiated into the mysteries of life, love and death.[15] The meaning of life is love, as proclaimed by Nuit who declares:

> For I am divided for love's sake, for the chance of union. This is the creation of the world, that the pain of division is as nothing, and the joy of dissolution all.[16]

The knowledge of life and love comes about through death, the medium of transformation. After such an eclipse has taken place in the dreaming inner landscape of the soul, 'that which remains' is the knowledge of ultimate reality gained from pure intellect:

> Remember all ye that existence is pure joy; that all the sorrows are but as shadows; they pass and are done; but there is that which remains.[17]

The world was created for love by the division of the soul and her spirit. It was created for the chance of their union. Death came into the world so that man could receive the spiritual knowledge of the True Will—the flame of love that burns within his heart, his real identity.

> I am the flame that burns in every heart of man, and in the core of every star. I am Life, and the giver of Life, yet therefore is the knowledge of me the knowledge of death.[18]

The book instructs the Initiate concerning the nature of this love, which is always returned to Nuit since she is its source. She repeatedly tells the Initiate that all love must be, 'To me', 'unto me', and 'always in the love of me'.[19]

---

[15] Thelema, 'Will', is written in Greek (Θελημα) in the Book of the Law I: 39, and may be pronounced *Theléma* (classical Greek) or *Theléma* (modern Greek), with the emphasis on the second syllable in both cases.
[16] I: 29–30.
[17] II: 9.
[18] II: 6.
[19] See I: 51–53, I: 61–63 and I: 65.

To fulfil this—the ultimate magical spell—the soul must know who Nuit is. She then understands this wilful aiming of the arrows of love 'for the chance of union'. Nuit describes herself thus:

> *Since I am Infinite Space, and the Infinite Stars thereof, do ye also thus. Bind nothing! Let there be no difference made among you between any one thing and any other thing; for thereby there cometh hurt.*[20]

The capitalisation reveals that Nuit here identifies herself with the goddess I.S.I.S. Space cannot be infinite as it is in manifestation and thus subject to determination. We must understand this as analogy, therefore, and not cosmological or spiritual fact. To 'bind' something traditionally relates to an oath used in certain magical practices, usually involving the evocation of subterranean demons (Asuras in Sanskrit). However, on the path of Knowledge there is no need to bind any inverse deity or *deva*—for evil spirits are precisely that. They simply cease to exist in the realisation of the Atma, which in the Book of the Law is called Hadit—though we must beware of the ambiguity of his Serpent aspect, which has a superior and inferior meaning. The instruction given by Nuit plainly applies to practices intended to support yogic Samadhi. It is most certainly not a rule by which any person can 'live out their life'; it is an instruction to the devotee. And what then, are these stars?

> *Every man and every woman is a star.*[21]

Clearly this does not imply 'everyman' or anyone, but it declares a truth. The 'star' as figured in Egyptian art is five-fingered or rayed. It is therefore an apt symbol comparable with the Sanskrit *jivatma* or 'creature self', reflective of the True Self or Atma. When concentrated in *jivatma*, and with all other objects of mind closed off completely, consciousness is aware of the ray of light from the higher intellect (Sanskrit *boddhi*). In the usual state of affairs, this is not known at all because the ego *centre* is the higher principle of the mind and its sensory faculties, which is all that is known, and at that vaguely, by the ordinary person.[22] By Greek number values, Thelema is identical to spiritual love:

---

[20] I: 22.
[21] I: 3.
[22] These technical matters are explained in *Thunder Perfect Gnosis*.

Thelema	(Will)	=	93
Agape	(Love)	=	93

We are given to understand that to 'love under will' is to love unto Nuit 'for the chance of union'.[23] That is, to partake of love that brings us to the joy of dissolution (Sanskrit *moksha*). Such love transcends even the spell of death, for it does not bind the soul to those creatures she loves. Instead, she achieves Hadit—the magical manifester of Nuit who gave separate existence for the chance of union. The dissolution, called *pralaya* in Sanskrit, is the ultimate goal of yoga and of the path of knowledge (*jnana*). It is therefore the love of pure knowledge for its own sake that is here figured, and not love in any ordinary sense of the word.

There is also a lesser path to consider. Such a lover is taken out of himself in ecstasy but he is not yet prepared for the inward journey. His soul is nonetheless able to move through creation, which is inclusive of all states of being in all worlds, informed by the True Will (*dharma*)—which transforms the soul it passes through, giving her substance. To 'take your fill and will of love as ye will, when, where and with whom ye will!' is to practice *karma* yoga, or the way of the householder and not the full time devotee. 'But always unto me' then means paying strict attention to rites and observances.[24] The conduct of the householder must be perfect in every way. Such a man must work for a living, so the chance of union may come eventually.

Wisdom discerns a difference between True Will and the personal will—which is a matter of determinations that amount to nothing in relation to the Real or the supreme principle. Likewise, one must discern a difference between the love of Nuit and the sensory, narcissistic love called Eros by the ancient Greeks—who understood Eros to be inseparable from Thanatos, death.[25] Hedonism or the satisfaction of Eros for its own sake leads to death, for it binds the life force of the natural soul to a body that is corruptible and perishable.

---

[23] See page 4.

[24] I: 51.

[25] Eros is here used to refer to sexual and narcissistic love, not to the principle of relatedness in human activities as the psychologist Carl Jung interpreted it. The desirous arrows fired from the bow of Eros are inseparable from the idea of fate, and consequently of death. The fated aspect of Eros owes to the passivity of will that is the condition of its usual mode of operation.

Thanatos, the dark shadow of Eros, refers not only to mortality but also metaphorically to the loss of spiritual life and love. It embodies the idea of the misery of the soul arising from sin, which begins on earth but lasts and increases after the death of the body in hell (or the underworld). In the widest sense it alludes to a tragedy even greater than this. Let us return again to the words of Nuit:

> *Bind nothing! Let there be no difference made between any one thing and any other thing; for thereby there cometh hurt.*[26]

This injunction against binding is given as a warning against the natural soul's tendency to bind things to herself, and therefore to finality and multiplicity, the world of differences between things. The bond of the love of Agape, on the other hand, does not bind things in nature thus causing finite differentiation. It unites them to that which is beyond visible nature. The purpose of the Great Work is to transform Eros, the natural love of the Scarlet Woman or soul, into a vehicle capable of overcoming the power of Thanatos. As we have previously established, Thelema or *love under will* is identical to the love called Agape by the ancient Greeks. Agape is that which remains after the death of the physical body, as opposed to Eros which—at best—merely vanishes away. What is left of man when he dies, if anything remains at all, is the love that has united him to the love of Nuit, a bond that endures beyond physical death. Agape is that love which binds souls together for the purpose of bringing them back to Nuit. Yet such a reward cannot be bargained for; in the final measure it is Nuit herself who chooses her lovers.

When Agape or *love under will* passes through the soul she is transfigured. If Eros alone animates her, then she is under the spell of its shadow Thanatos. She cuts herself off from her spiritual destiny. She then suffers progressive degradation and loss of substance, which is not a punishment but merely 'how things are', natural law. This must not in any way be understood as a moral consequence. No one would attach moral significance to the fact of a rotten apple falling from a tree in a storm. The way of the Initiate is not about following arbitrary rules or conditions that are supposed to be 'lived up to'.

---

[26] I: 22.

The natural soul or *prima materia* must therefore be torn apart or dissembled by the wheels set in motion by initiatic transmission. Dying the 'death' of an Initiate, which means turning her face from wordly things, she returns that which sprang from the source of Nuit, which is her True Self. Only then is she able to break open the shell of her separate existence. The Law of Thelema calls her to silence the empty echo of her own voice so that she may know the beauty of Nuit:

> *Also for beauty's sake and love's!*[27]

There follows immediately an instruction:

> *Invoke me under my stars! Love is the law, love under will. Nor let the fools mistake love; for there are love and love. There is the dove, and there is the serpent. Choose ye well.*[28]

Spiritual and profane love are to be the subject of discrimination. The love and worship of Nuit, for the practitioner that still requires magical means as a support to initiation, is to be understood as nocturnal. That is, it does not take place in the ordinary waking conscious mode attributed to the day but in the fleeting, tenuous and oftentimes elusive shadow realm of night wherein the real and the imagined are no longer contradictory. Yet the conscious (or solar) will is to play a vital part in this, for Nuit is known not only by discerning when, where and with whom to love, but also by choosing *how* to love. The choice is to be made wisely. Suppression is no better than self-indulgence. If the soul silences the flesh by an act of violence, the flesh will take revenge upon the soul, secretly infecting her with a spirit of rebellion. It is an error to suppose that spiritual life is a mere negation of matter. By the use of magick, everything we have to offer—mind body and soul—is to serve the Great Work. In this way, the principle of life itself is sought above and beyond the deceptive human nature. The one that has attained Hadit, the giver of Life, enjoys the world loving all things without attachment, in perfect freedom. Hadit reminds the practitioner of *karma* yoga:

> *Be not animal; refine thy rapture!*[29]

---

[27] III: 56.
[28] I: 57.
[29] II: 70.

Hadit thereby invites the soul to fully experience all the joys of the earthly existence, calling forth man's lust as a means of knowing the joys that inebriate the soul. This way takes a long time and the soul may need to pass through many states of being or worlds before the goal can be realised.

> *I am the Snake that giveth Knowledge and Delight and bright glory, and stir the hearts of men with drunkenness. To worship me take wine and strange drugs whereof I will tell my prophet, and be drunk thereof! They shall not harm ye at all. It is a lie, this folly against self. The exposure of innocence is a lie. Be strong, o man! lust, enjoy all things of sense and rapture: fear not that any God shall deny thee for this.*[30]

The above verse has led many souls to damnation. It is couched in very ambiguous terms, so that a person may interpret it any way they want, including a kind of license to indulge in activities that are very destructive to body and mind. From the point of Hadit as the Atma supreme, it makes no difference what happens to the body or mind. It makes a good deal of difference to the human being, for the chance of liberation can be lost forever through such foolishness. We may also interpret this 'drunkenness' as the spiritual kind of intoxication, which belongs to Nuit herself, and who urges her lovers thus:

> *I love you! I yearn to you! Pale or purple, veiled or voluptuous, I who am all pleasure and purple, and drunkenness of the innermost sense, desire you. Put on the wings, and arouse the coiled splendour within you: come unto me!*[31]

The latter verse is unambiguous. The Thelemite desires only ecstasy that frees the soul. The 'wine' that so inebriates the soul is divine and has nothing to do with any ordinary kind of pleasure.

> *Obey my prophet! follow out the ordeals of my knowledge! seek me only! Then the joys of my love will redeem ye from all pain. This is so: I swear it by the vault of my body; by my sacred heart and tongue; by all I can give, by all I desire of ye all.*[32]

Obedience to the path is required. The 'prophet' is Hadit (Atma). Redemption is the lesser path but preferable to death as finality.

---

[30] II: 22.

[31] I: 61.

[32] I: 32.

The Hermetic Great Work

With the passing of time the face of eternity takes on new expressions in human consciousness. As the World Soul passes through her cyclical changes, so the divine Word or Logos modifies his utterance to preserve creation from inertia. Nothing in the universe remains static; likewise, the relationship between God and man has its phases of development.

Spiritual law is Universal, as expressed through all ancient traditions. It has been continued exoterically, through the symbolism alone, in the West over the last two millennia: to be redeemed from suffering and death, man must sacrifice his personal will to that of God. Yet through the ages, what is revealed to mankind about the mysteries of the life of his soul undergoes transformation. When the ancient Egyptian tradition withdrew and disappeared to all intents and purposes, alchemy and Hermeticism were thrown out like seeds and scattered throughout the world. Death is overcome by fixing the volatile, that is, by the transfiguration of the mutable elements of the natural soul.

For those called to follow the path of initiation, the Absolute is the unfathomable depth beyond all of creation and cosmos. God, as the expression of this Absolute, is the androgynous binary intelligence begetting all the possibilities of existence. These in turn preserve the equilibrium of the universe. The dual aspect of the eternal is named after the Egyptian gods Nuit and Hadit. Nuit and Hadit are identical to the Mother and Son of the ancient mysteries that predate the notion of God as 'Father'. Nuit is—seen from the outward point of view—the goddess of space and stars, while Hadit is her manifester, her Word and Will, her heart and her tongue.[33] He is the contraction or limit that begets individual consciousness.[34] The body of Nuit is 'heaven', in which each individual centre of consciousness is a 'star':

The unveiling of the company of heaven.
Every man and every woman is a star.[35]

---

[33] This view is outward because the Absolute does not act directly upon manifestation. It is the 'unmoved mover' as previously mentioned.
[34] As the begetter of the soul, Hadit is the inferior form of the Serpent, who takes on a demiurgic rôle—like Satan, he is an inverse reflection of God.
[35] I: 2–3.

Divine Intelligence appears, though strictly from the limited human and earthly point of view, as a begetter of change and multiplicity who assumes many names. This was well known to the ancients but not to modern commentators, who imagine that all pre-religious civilisations were polytheistic. The different forms of deity refer to particular attributes and powers, all expressions of primordial Unity, from which manifestation comes about through self-polarisation.

> *None, breathed the light, faint and faery, of the stars, and two.*
> *For I am divided for love's sake, for the chance of union.*
> *This is the creation of the world, that the pain of division is as nothing, and the joy of dissolution all.*[36]

The ancient Egyptians represented begetting (and so multiplicity) by the power of division. While neither numbers or stars, or space as the field of containment, are truly infinite as they owe to manifestation, numbers and mathematics can serve as an analogy to help our minds grasp what is otherwise unknowable. René Guénon has given us a simple and very clear example:[37]

> All the numbers can be considered to emanate from within Unity in pairs; these pairs of inverse or complementary numbers, which may be regarded as symbolising the syzygies of the Aeons of the Pleroma, exist within Unity in the undifferentiated or non-manifest state:
>
> $$1 = 1/2 \times 2 = 1/3 \times 3 = 1/4 \times 4 = 1/5 \times 5 = \ldots = 0 \times \infty$$
>
> None of these groups, $1/n \times n$, is distinct from Unity, or from the other groups within Unity; they become so only when their constituent elements are considered separately; it is then that Duality is born, distinguishing one principle from the other, not in opposition, as is ordinarily—and wrongly—said, but as complementary principles, active and passive, positive and negative, masculine and feminine, But the two principles coexist within Unity, and their indivisible duality itself constitutes a secondary unity, a reflection of primordial Unity; thus together with the Unity that contains them, the two complementary elements compose the Ternary, which is the first manifestation of Unity, for two, being the issue of one, cannot exist without three thereby existing as well:
>
> $$1 + 2 = 3$$

---

[36] I: 28–30. Note that the preceding verse I: 27 is a poetic intervention by Crowley, and which is doctrinally incorrect. We do not comment on it here.
[37] René Guénon, 'On the Production of Numbers', from *Miscellanea*.

The multiplication by division continues until the Pythagorean Decad is obtained, which is the most complete expression of manifestation:

$$1 + 2 + 3 + 4 = 10$$

That can also be expressed: $\sum (1-4) = 10$. The Pythagorean Numbers are called 'triangular', as all of them can fit perfectly into a triangle:

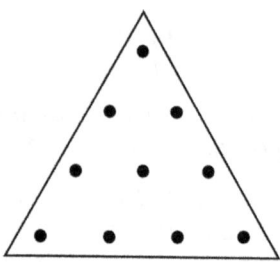

The Pythagorean model was affirmed in a riddle near the end of the Book of the Law, though this does not seem to have been realised by Crowley or his followers. According to Liber AL, III: 73:

> *Paste the sheets from right to left and from top to bottom: then behold!*

There are 66 sheets of the holograph manuscript in total; the arrangement here is a pyramid with a base of eleven—if the capstone is counted as zero the pyramid expresses $\sum (0-11) = 66$.

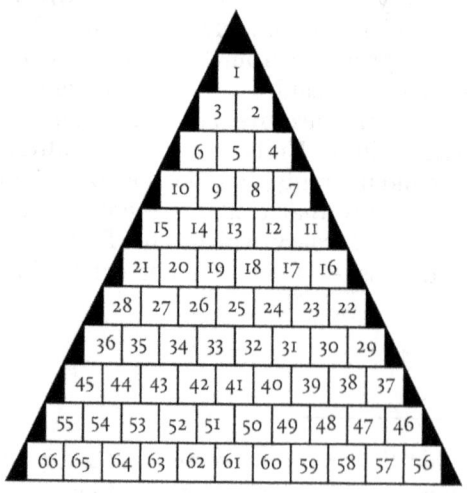

We thus behold a calculator for the Pythagorean numbers from 1 to 11. The number eleven expresses perfect harmony of the macrocosm and microcosm and is therefore a number of the Great Work. The numbers in the squares down the left side, 1, 3, 6, 10 … are the Pythagorean numbers, the rows are their means of calculation.

According to René Guénon, the conversion of all Quality into Quantity at the end of the Age of Kali Yuga (i.e., the present time) may be represented by a triangle (and so also a pyramid).[38] The capstone then represents perfect Unity and the supreme principle. The tenth numbered row represents the totality of all possibilities of manifestation, as does $\sum (1-10) = 55$. The eleventh row at the base then has a dual aspect: In one respect it is the Qliphoth or World of Shades, for it is barely in manifestation at all and so represents the *sub-infra* states of being, which are the natural abode of the System of Antichrist. Pure Quantity can never actually come about as the world would cease to manifest, but as we near the end of the Age of Kali Yuga, there is an increasing tendency towards it. As the number 11 also represents perfect unity, we can see that as soon as Pure Quantity is nearly realised, the world ceases to be in manifestation as does the present race of humans. The *mahapralaya* withdraws all in dissolution. In an instant (simultaneously), the next Manvantara comes about in the cyclical series.

The meaning in the verses from Liber AL, I: 28—30 is that 'none and two' can be used as an analogy for the metaphysical Zero. This is not to be thought of as 'nothing', for it contains All. The metaphysical 'point', which is used as a symbol for Unity (the number one is only a representation), is anciently conceived as luminous, perfect and whole, indivisible. Thus the solar symbol ☉ can represent Nuit and Hadit as the summation of all these ideas expressed. The forms apprehended by consciousness conceal the Hidden One who is able to manifest by the power of 'none and two'. The Hidden One is a name of the principal Theban god Amoun, who sets or sinks as the Sun below the horizon of waking consciousness. He is referred to as 'Amen' in Liber AL, II: 49, which is a form often used by Egyptologists. We have previously decribed the work of magick as 'nocturnal', for its operations are primarily in the subtle domain, which consciousness inhabits in the dreaming state. The idea is not to be detained in the underworld but to pass through it, however, leaving the body at rest.

---

[38] *The Reign of Quantity and the Signs of the Times* [Sophia Perennis].

Manifested existence itself is a perennial process of self-renewal; the universe finds stability through change—through the constant making and breaking of identities. Like the *ouroboros*, the great serpent that eats its own tail, and the pelican that feeds its children on its own blood, life periodically consumes itself to be recreated.

This shall regenerate the world, the little world my sister, my heart and my tongue, unto whom I send this kiss.[39]

The Initiate is called to understand a primary duality: the infinity veiled by the form of Nuit, who is manifested by Hadit, her Word, her sacred heart or star. To be informed by Hadit, the soul or Scarlet Woman must receive the communication from Horus or Ra Hoor Khuit. By the power of his magick Hadit sends forth Horus, and the result is a polarisation of consciousness:

Now let it be first understood that I am a god of War and Vengeance. I shall deal hardly with them.[40]

Liber AL vel Legis is a book of the Last Judgement, the ultimate initiatory trial and final transformation passed through by the soul. Thelema must then involve a testing and weighing of the heart in what can at least appear to be a considerable spiritual ordeal.[41] Such ordeals may be subtle and not even realised by the aspirant. The ambiguous nature of the Thelemic source text lends itself easily to the idiocy of fundamentalist interpretation. It is a book to listen to with the heart; reason alone is fated to suffer its curses. The book declares that, 'the exposure of innocence is a lie'; its effect is to strip the soul naked before the unrelenting eye of Horus, the Avenging Angel.[42] The Last Judgement operates on three levels. Firstly, it makes possible the preparation of the soul for initiation, which is to understand that all the joys of this world are balanced equally by suffering. The second level involves the spiritual overcoming of physical death, which constitutes a 'second birth' (into spirit). Both of these levels are individual.

---

[39] I: 53.

[40] III: 3.

[41] An ordeal cannot be spiritual, properly speaking, as all trials pertain only to the contingencies of the ordinary life of a man, and vanish to nothing in the light of the realisation that is Gnosis (Sanskrit *jnana*).

[42] II: 22.

The third level is universal since it involves total transcendance of the individuality and final liberation (*moksha*), which is reflected in the dissolution that takes place at the end of each greater Cosmic Cycle (Manvantara). The Last Judgement presents itself at the end of a great period of time from the terrestrial point of view, which is also the apotheosis of degradation in terms of the human consciousness. Individuals nonetheless have unique possibilities and even at the end of time some may recover their memory of what is real and true and even obtain direct knowledge, as did the seers of old times. This may at times give rise to fierce battles. The Initiate must be well prepared for such encounters, which means being prepared for face-to-face confrontation with all the potentiality for good and evil within the soul. Thelema is therefore 'the law of the strong'.[43] The Great Work of returning the soul to the love and joy of Nuit is nonetheless its primary aim. The Law of Thelema is thus universal because it is so particular, once it is fully understood:

Do what thou wilt shall be the whole of the Law.[44]

As with some of the previous instructions, this is not something that everyman or anyone can achieve. The nearest doctrinal equivalent to the True Will is the Sanskrit *dharma*, which unfortunately has no translation in any modern language in one or two words. Dharma can be on a group or collective level, as with a race or civilisation, and it can also be that of an individual. It means doing and thinking what is in perfect accordance with the spiritual supreme principle, as that is modified in its expression through each manifest being. While the statement above appears to be all about action (*karma*), 'doing', the most ultimate action in spiritual terms is non-action, which means being very much like the 'unmoved mover', Hadit (or Atma). It does not mean living out an earthly life and doing nothing! Obviously, that is impossible. It means that all thoughts and deeds are entirely without attachment. In truth, it is unlikely there are more than a few persons in the world today that could follow out this aspect of Thelema, for one would have to be what is called in the yoga method of Patañjali a Dharmamegha *yogin*. Such a person has attained the final liberation, or is otherwise very near it, while still alive on earth.

---

[43] II: 21.
[44] I: 40.

Another term for this is Jivanmukta, 'fully liberated while still communicating as an individual person', or at least that is how it appears to men.[45] To have any chance of this, or of getting anywhere near it—for it is the supreme ideal of the (Egyptian) Book of the Law—the Initiate must transcend the ideologies of the modern world that are the product of a deformed mentality, producing the evils of self-righteousness and tyrannical repression. These evils are hidden to ordinary men, for they seem to be all about equality, diversity, 'social responsibility' and so forth.[46] The System of Antichrist even produces fake spirituality and pseudo-initiatic or even anti-initiatic organisations. Those who follow these suffer increasing restriction, owing to the complete absence of principial knowledge and confused idealism originating from the contamination of political interests, which automatically cancel out all spiritual possibilities whatsoever. As Nuit so concisely whispers to her followers:[47]

The word of Sin is Restriction.[48]

Thus initiation puts earthly existence in a new perspective. To know the infinite is to pass beyond the suffering and sorrow that inevitably result from identification with the finite.

Remember all ye that existence is pure joy; that all the sorrows are but as shadows; they pass and are done; but there is that which remains.[49]

---

[45] An adept (in the real sense) can form different minds and even bodies to communicate with humans. This may seem astonishing to some but it is a part of orthodox Hinduism, accounted for in scriptures and commentaries.

[46] The general public retain an obsolete notion of what totalitarianism really is. Most still think it is about dictators and political parties. The System of Antichrist works across all political idealism in the world today. Equality is impossibility while diversity forces everyone to be the same, as differences are only tolerated so long as the same values are accepted. See 'Uniformity against Unity', *Thunder Perfect Gnosis*.

[47] The followers of Nuit are expressly *not* the followers of the cult of the Beast as designed by Crowley and those who continue his institutionalised mockery of all spiritual knowledge and traditions.

[48] I: 41.

[49] II: 9.

The Beast and Leviathan

The Golden Dawn founder, S.L. MacGregor Mathers, provided us with a coherent explanation of the doctrine of the Qliphoth in his translation of *Sepher Dtzenioutha*.[50] The commentary is luminous but it is not composed in a way that is accessible to the modern reader. The Qabalistic doctrine of the Qliphoth or 'Evil Shells of Matter' uses the symbolism of the Dragon or Leviathan. At the base of the Tree of Life, below or otherwise entwined about Malkuth, the shells are 'under the form of a vast serpent extending this way and that'.[51] The implication is that mortal man is under the shadow of what is called 'extreme justice' or severity.[52] This defines the material world, where we are placed under absolute restriction or confinement by our own physical and sensory inclination. Beyond that, extending upward from Malkuth to the Abyss, the human psyche is similarly under a great force of restriction, though it is deemed as less severe than the deep pit of that which is wholly material, and which admits to no spiritual reality whatsoever. That most inferior form of the Beast or Dragon typifies the mentality that shapes today's world, and which is now governed by what we have termed the System of Antichrist.

The psychic force, which has its operation in the subtle domain, and which prevails over the intermediary realms between heaven and earth, or between the spiritual and substantial, is likened to a great sea-serpent, or 'that great dragon which is in the sea'. This dragon is said to have a single nostril (aperture) 'after the manner of whales', so that it is able to receive the influence or *mezla* from the worlds beyond the Abyss.[53] And this is the meaning of Psalms, 74: 13, where it is said,

Thou hast broken the heads of the dragons upon the waters.

---

[50] Mather's translation of Knorr Von Rosenroth, *Kabbalah Unveiled*, line 25.
[51] Ibid.
[52] This term is used in the Enochian Calls of the Aethyrs.
[53] Mathers [*ibid*].

The subject is unavoidably technical; this dragon (or dragons, for it encompasses two) is a universal symbol that sums up the seven planetary sephiroth or mundane chakras as dependent from Binah. These are seen Qabalistically as inferior or lower *emanations* of that Throne of the Supernal Wisdom. The 'bruised head' of the serpent is Da'ath, the Ogdoad, the highest point that the normal intellectual and moral faculties of man can obtain before the Great Sea of Binah, the wisdom born of the Intelligible Light.

The other dragon referred to is that of the lower subtle regions, which form a magnetic belt, as it were, about the earth. This dragon is bound up in Malkuth, and is under the presidency of the Tav or Tau Cross of the thirty-second path that joins Malkuth with the Foundation, also known as the sphere of the Moon. The path is attributed to Saturn, Lord of Time. Human consciousness is bound fast to the time process in the normal state of affairs, even as Malkuth, the world, is symbolically cut off from the rest of the Tree by the coils of the dragon. Thus, there is an abyss of height and an abyss of depth; naturally these reflect one another. For example, the sephira Binah (Intelligible) and non-sephira Da'ath (Knowledge)—which is secreted within her—are attributed to the mundane chakra or sphere of Saturn, as is the path of the Tav (ת). However, they exist on different planes, above and below, of heaven and the earth, and should not be confused.[54]

Comparison may be made with the dismemberment of Osiris by Set or Saturn. Osiris, as a consequence of the trick played on him by Set, had to undergo death, being bereft of the immortal principle as symbolised by the phallus of Osiris or 'lost word'. He was then made subject to time. The phallus or rejected immortal principle of Osiris was cast, it was said, into the Nile where it was swallowed by a fish, or otherwise lost at sea. This obtains on more than one level, as we shall explain. According to the Hindu doctrine of the Cosmic Cycles, Vishnu assumed the form of a fish at the end of the last great Manvantara. He told Manu, Lord of the Manvantara, that he would carry the seeds of the great cycle over to form the new Manvantara cycle after the great deluge.[55] Thus on the microcosmic scale, the mind of man may resurrect as Horus, the divine 'child' of Isis so the immortal principle may be restored through the power of love.

---

[54] A simple presentation of the Tree of Life, the sephiroth and paths, is given in our book *Hermetic Qabalah Foundation—Complete Course*.
[55] See 'Cosmic Cycles', *Nu Hermetica*.

In the concave head of the Dragon then, the phallic power is withdrawn so that the feminine principle can obtain. To use the Taoist terminology, the sage must become *yin* to the *yang* of the primordial principle, so that earth and heaven may be reunited. The soul is able to 'give birth to herself', or in other terms, accomplish the miracle of resurrection. It is the rôle and function of Isis to give life, for she is life itself, and the breath of life, the *ankh*, seat, throne or foundation of all that can exist.

The Qliphoth, 'shells' or so-called demons, are therefore no more than inverse and distorted forms of the sephiroth of the Tree of Life. The sephiroth hold the dual function of transmitting and receiving, for they receive higher influence and transmit it to the emanations below. The 'nostril' of the dragon is its receptivity as opposed to its horn or crest, which is active and penetrative. When the dragon's head is broken upon the waters and the crest is made receptive or concave then all conceptual thoughts, numbers or emanations, are seen to emerge from and fall back into the mind that produced them. This is no different than Raja Yoga, where it corresponds to the stage where the concentration of mind shuts down all mental processes to be fixed on the unity of the mind of God (or Shakti) and the goal, or at least the primary one, is reached, which is called Samadhi.

The nature of Saturn (or Set) is concentration. The translation of the penetrative horn of the dragon into a receptive vessel allows the possibility of a miraculous Flower of Mind, from which may emerge the divine 'child', Horus. The dual modes or functions of expansion and contraction are therefore both necessary for the realisation of spiritual consciousness. However, if one over-uses the concentration faculty of the dragon or becomes bound up by it, the result is a hardening, the forming of a shell-like exterior; in other words, the mind is not then capable of receptivity to the spiritual influence.

This is why it is said that some persons are suitable for initiation while others are not, for when the shells have tightened their grip so as to completely seal off the doors to heaven, so to speak, that person is impervious to initiation. It is impossible for them to understand even the outer mysteries of symbol and allegory. Profane scholarship, philosophy and science alike do not only encourage such hardening, but also positively exalt it and, by its easy domination of the lower worlds and the minds of the ignorant, it is used to gain power and influence through total denial of spiritual realities.

One of the clearest doctrinal fragments of Liber AL vel Legis sums up the dual nature of the Serpent or Dragon, whose power can bring wisdom to the wise and ignorance to the foolish. This Serpent Power is identical to that force linked with the Shakti power in the Hindu Tantras, and spells out the dangers of all such practices:

> *I am the secret Serpent coiled about to spring: in my coiling there is joy. If I lift up my head, I and my Nuit are one. If I droop down mine head, and shoot forth venom, then is rapture of the earth, and I and the earth are one.*
>
> *There is a great danger in me; for who doth not understand these runes shall make a great miss. He shall fall down into the pit called Because, and there he shall perish with the dogs of Reason.*[56]

The soul whose desire to bond for completion is not informed by the True Will but is mislead by her reason or controlling ego, perishes in the Abyss, the 'pit called Because'. In Indian tradition, no person would attempt to practice Kundalini Yoga, or any form of yoga, without first obtaining a guru willing to help them. As for magick, which consists of various applications of traditional sciences, only in modern times, and particularly in the West, would it become possible that so many persons, believing in the illogicality of 'self-initiation' would lead themselves and others into total self-delusion.

Without the power of concentration there can be no ascent, no elevation of consciousness. Having arisen, one must not presume oneself Lord of All, as do the tyrants of the world.[57] One must be receptive to spiritual influence. Dissolution of the egoistic counterfeit of reality is here implied, for man's reason cannot penetrate beyond the objects created by his own mind. The premature use of the receptive mode, on the other hand, results in a gradual wasting away and dispersion of the soul for there can then be no involvement with spiritual or initiatic transmission.[58]

---

[56] II: 26–27.

[57] Such tyrants climb an inverse hierarchy, of which the 'pinnacle' is the pit of Satan—the 'top' is therefore the bottom, regarded spiritually.

[58] See Guénon, *Perspectives on Initiation*, Chapters 21 and 22, where the magical powers are explained very thoroughly [Sophia Perennis].

By 'premature', we refer to the excessive use of the receptive mode before sufficient knowledge and experience has been built into the structure of the individuality, making the mind flexible and thereby capable of operating according to both modes of function at will. The consequence of such an error, which is sadly very common among those who seek something vaguely spiritual but refuse to take up the discipline and work of an initiatic Order (assuming they can find one), is much the same in the end result as that of the Saturnian contraction. The person is ultimately bound to the planes of illusion, captivated by the magnetic force called variously Leviathan or Beast. It must be said also that this is frequently the case with 'psychics', and those who would, as a matter of habit or preference, place far too high a value on the magical powers (so-called). And although there are many of these who would not think of themselves as psychics as such, and may not even believe that the subtle plane exists in its own degree of reality, these have nonetheless over-developed certain very particular magical or otherwise purely imaginative functions. The latter are more dangerous than the psychics for they retain an active will that is invariably turned towards evil, if they know it or not.

There is a further symbolic aspect of the dragon to consider. The serpent holding its tail in its mouth forms a circle—the serpent of Saturn, *ouroboros*. In his action upon Malkuth, the material world, he is not only the executor of judgment but he is also the Destroyer. His power is therefore that of destruction as opposed to creation, death as opposed to life. Furthermore, this dragon is concealed. He is only known through irregularity or disequilibrium. In that case, his appearance is as the accuser, or the executor of judgment, and it is for this reason he is known as the Destroyer. Spiritual realisation nonetheless requires destruction of the previous state, and that is why many seekers of that which they think of as initiation baulk no sooner they come anywhere near contacting the spiritual forces that would undo them. The slightest degree of contact is only perceived in their minds as an overwhelming accusatory force. In self-protection, they turn against those who would help them if they were brave enough to attempt to master the acquisitive force in them. The human ego (*ahankara*) becomes destructive or separative when it mistakes sensorial impressions for the true Self. According to Advaita, the senses are 'the slayers of the Real'. The power is turned against itself, so to speak, for reality to be known.

A priest makes a 'sacrifice' so that he becomes a word made perfect, a truth-speaker such as Ankh-af-na-khonsu. The sacrifice is only a preparation for real initiation that involves irreversible change in the state of the being. The translation of the *Stele of Revealing*, given in Liber AL, III: 37, is questionable:

For me unveils the veiléd sky, the self-slain Ankh-af-na-khonsu.

The office and real function of Ankh-af-na-khonsu as the 'opener of the doors of heaven' means he had not only made the priestly sacrifice but was also an intermediary between Heaven and Earth, the principle and the manifested state. He was as one who ascends and descends the ladder of the stars or worlds. The Egyptian words *ma'a kheru* mean, 'Whose word is true (before the Gods)'. The 'self-slain' notion derives from a misunderstanding of the hieroglyph *kheru*. It is thought to be a sacrificial block, but is used in this context as a phonetic, not a determinative. Also, whether it really does symbolise a 'sacrificial block' is open to question. Comparison with other hieroglyphs suggests it may symbolise the door to a shrine—which more accurately reflects the priestly rôle and function.

The ass, a Setian creature, must be prepared to carry the ark, which is to say we must be prepared to submit egoistic pride to that which is above and beyond us. Set, a strange creature-symbol that was carried over to Egypt from the Atlantean tradition, is usually depicted as having truncated ears.[59] However, on the two pillars of the festival hieroglyph for the king's thirty or (subsequently) three-year Jubilee, Set is shown at the head of the right-hand pillar with unusually elongated (thus receptive) ears.[60] At the head of the left-hand pillar, Set is depicted wearing the symbol of Ma'at, 'Truth'—for he is here fully justified. Likewise, the name of IAI, the Ass god, is spelled with the plumes of Ma'at.[61]

---

[59] The Atlantean tradition preceded the present Great Year commencing with the precessional Age of Leo. The 'sinking of Atlantis', whether a fact of history or a symbolic allusion to the ending of a complete world and the start of a new one, coincided more or less with the melting of the glaciers that brough the last Ice Age to a premature conclusion.
[60] Both 30 and 3 correspond to Saturn, the formative principle. Thirty is an approximation of the number of years it takes Saturn to complete a round of the zodiacal circle. Binah is the third emanation and the Mother of Form.
[61] See 'The Ass of God', *Nu Hermetica*. Also our *Egyptian Tarot* trump XXI.

The Sphinx: Symbol of Love and Will

The Law of Thelema relates the mysteries of a God who, being both none and two, conceives through parthenogenesis. As two, the divine androgyne is the means of manifest expression of all the possibilities of existence. One may make fruitful comparison with Adam Kadmon in the Hebraic tradition, and the Universal Man of the Arabs. One must also beware of taking the term 'androgyne' as a sign of an anthropomorphic God, for Universal Being is not a human being.

Hidden at the heart of creation, the enigmatic Word is a shape-shifter. He and the world he creates around him take on new forms over time, and the pattern of their transformation is marked by periodicity. The Cosmic Cycles return, as when following the curve or circumference of a circle, but never replicate; thus the analogous shape for the worlds of manifestation is spiralic. Although Nuit is eternal and immutable, her Will in creation depends upon time and space from the particular human point of view. Nothing in creation is absolute as it is by nature subject to determination. Nonetheless, some things are truly ordained whilst others miss the mark, being out of time, out of place and without love.[62]

The begetter of change takes on many names, each a word or form displayed to the soul to help her understand her true nature. Thus she is able to consciously participate in the universal life cycle while remaining united to Hadit. The means of so doing is referred to in Liber AL vel Legis as the Beast—which is illogical unless we first remove the obfuscation of Crowley, who personally identified with the Beast of Revelation. Thus, sometimes the book addresses him as 'Beast' while at other times it is made clear he is not in any way the Lord of any Cosmic Cycle, as it is impossible for any human being to be that—the human is by definition subject to determination:

> *For he is ever a sun, and she a moon. But to him is the winged secret flame, and to her the stooping starlight.*
> *But ye are not so chosen.*[63]
>
> *... in these are mysteries that no Beast shall divine.*[64]

---

[62] The social and political ideologies mentioned on the last page of 'The Hermetic Great Work', for example, are *adharmic*—without *dharma*.
[63] I: 16–17.
[64] III: 47.

In ancient Egyptian iconography, the Logos takes on countless forms. He was known as Hu, the Sphinx, and sometimes Hormaku. Liber AL vel Legis uses the Greek variant of this name: Hrumachis. Many names and forms are alluded to in the book, such as the hawk-headed Ra, Heru-ra-ha, Ra Hoor Khuit and the man-child Hoor-paar-kraat. Other forms of the solar principle include Tum, the beetle Khephra and the woman Ahathoor (or Hathoor). These gods are all expressions of the solar, transformative power of Mind hidden in creation yet animating it.

The Sphinx is the most ancient symbol of the androgynous and polymorphous god to be found on earth today. Hrumachis is an aspect of Horus, who, like the sun, perpetually arises renewed from his journey through the cycle of creation. He is also more than that, for he is able to attain deliverance (*moksha*).

Hrumachis is closely related to the extremely ancient god Bes, who is represented by a dwarf. Bes, 'the aged one who makes himself young again', was figured in early Egyptian dynasties; by the time of the New Kingdom he became identified with Horus the child, Hoor paar kraat. Little by little, Bes was identified with other forms of the Sun god such as Horus, Ra and Tum, until at length he absorbed their qualities. As such, Bes moved into a closer relationship with Hrumachis. By the XXVIth dynasty (663 to 525 BC) Bes was merged completely with Horus, with whom he shared the attribute of Lord of all Typhonian Beasts.

With a lion's body and a human face, the Sphinx represents both love (and so wisdom) and power. As such, the Sphinx is the embodiment of the union of sacerdotal authority, the head, which does not act but rests in contemplation, and temporal power, the body of the lion or Beast, which is upheld by the king, the nobility and warrior caste. The attitude of the Sphinx as resting indicates peace, always the ideal. The king is nonetheless able to act if action is needed to restore justice or equilibrium. Thus the Sphinx is the perfect symbol of love and law, wisdom and strength, peace and justice. She is more than that too, as we shall see. It is worth quoting at length from A.K. Coomaraswamy in this respect:[65]

---

[65] *Guardians of the Sun Door* by Ananda Kentish Coomaraswamy, Chapter VIII, Conclusion. We have here abridged the text and adjusted the spelling in places, for consistency.

Mercy and Majesty are precisely the two aspects of the Logos which are represented by the guardian Cherubim of the Old Testament. This is the unifying Logos as the Spirit, Light or Word of God-that-Is, and who is median in two ways, both inasmuch as he stands (like the apex of a triangle in relation to its other angles) above and between the creative-beneficent and royal-legislative Powers, represented by the Cherubim, dividing them and all other opposites from one another, and inasmuch as He stands on the border (μεθοπιος) 'between the extremes of the created and uncreated', acting as mediator—suppliant on man's behalf and ambassador on that of the Father, and like the Sun, whose place is that of the fourth in the middle of the seven planets. The centrality of the solar Logos corresponds to that of the Indian Breath (*prana*) or Universal Fire (Agni Vaishvānara) or Supernal Sun—not the sun that all men see, but the Sun of the Sun, the Light of Lights, as the Vedas and Plato express it. Furthermore, by a consideration of the verb σφιγυω from which the noun 'Sphinx' comes, we have been led to think of the Sphinx as a manifestation of the principle that joins all things together in a common nexus, and of that luminous, pneumatic, etherial thread of the Spirit by which God draws all things unto Himself by an irresistable attraction.

—This 'irresistable attraction' has been mentioned earlier in the text in relation to the *sutratma*, 'golden thread', ray of the *sushumna* and so forth. It is both the weave of worlds and that which can bring us into union with both Cosmos, God and ultimate Reality.

By the Sphinx is meant the Harmony of the Universe: Harmony is here almost as if it were the name of the Goddess, and with reference to the root meaning of the word, 'to join together', like the carpenter whom we—more literally—term a 'joiner'. I need not tell you that Christ was also a carpenter (αρμοστης) in just that sense, or that every form of the Artificer 'through whom all things were made' must be a carpenter wherever we think of the stuff of which the world was made as a 'wood' (υλη, or in Sanskrit *vana*). So the Sphinx, despite her femininity which corresponds to that of the divine Nature, can be regarded as a type of Christ, or more precisely, like the Dove, as a figure of the Spirit in motion, for it is by it that he draws them to Himself. The Sphinx, in other words, is Love; and though rather in the image of Aphrodite than in that of Eros, mother and son were originally hardly distinguishable in character or function. If you ask, 'Is not the Sphinx also the symbol of Death?' need I but remind you that in all traditions Love and Death are one and the same Person, or that God has said of Himself in many scriptures that 'I slay and make alive'?

The lion and the woman are symbols of the astrological signs of Leo and Aquarius, the 'Star and the Snake' of Liber AL.[66] The Star and Snake are Nuit and Hadit, dual aspects of the divine androgyne. Of Hrumachis, there will be more to tell, for the wheel of the aeons accelerated towards its dissolution with the dawning of the twenty-first century. Hrumachis has arisen at the 'fall of the Great Equinox', which signifies a fatal separation from spirit:

> *But your holy place shall be untouched throughout the centuries: though with fire and sword it be burnt down and shattered, yet an invisible house there standeth, and shall stand until the fall of the Great Equinox; when Hrumachis shall arise and the double-wanded one assume my throne and place.*[67]

By the tropical (or solar) Zodiac the Sun always enters the sign of Aries at the spring equinox, and that of Libra at the autumn equinox. However by the sidereal (or stellar) Zodiac, the Sun now enters the sign of Aquarius at the spring equinox and Leo at the autumn equinox. This is the fall of the Great Equinox, for the precessional Great Year of 13,000 years—half of a complete precessional cycle—begins at Leo the Lion, according to the wisdom tradition of the ancient Egyptians.[68] We are now at the 'fall' or autumn of the Great Year and the end of an entire Manvantara of four Yugas, of which the present Age of Kali is the last.[69] Thus all of time ends at this 'fall', and any continuance of the journey by the soul is nocturnal, out of time, and requires first passing through the hell of the underworld. While alive on earth this means recognising fully the tricks and deceptions of the System of Antichrist. Those who fall under the spell of that 'beast' are doomed to perish, for the ultimate delusion is to imagine that man is supreme and there is no God and no other reality but the world of man's imagining.

---

[66] 'The Sun, Strength and Sight, Light; these are for the servants of the Star and the Snake' (II: 21).

[67] III: 34. It is curious that on the night of the winter solstice, 22nd December 2015, Boleskine Manor, the place that Aleister Crowley called his 'holy place', his 'Kiblah', on the shores of Loch Ness in Scotland, burnt down to the ground and was almost completely destroyed by the fire. There is no particular reason to think this is in any way significant but it seems worthwhile mentioning it.

[68] Cf. 'Knights of the Cross', *The Way of Knowledge*.

[69] For a concise but clear explanation of the complex Cosmic Cycles of the Hindu *puranas* and other books, see *Nu Hermetica*. For more detail, see the book *Traditional Forms and Cosmic Cycles*, René Guénon.

Humanity has fully entered the time of Apocalypse as cryptically revealed—and concealed—in the book. The Fall of the Great Equinox has come and the star of Hrumachis or Hormaku has arisen. The event will mean very little to the human race as a whole, who will carry on their business as they always do, although none can escape the inevitable. The book of Revelation of St. John, also known as the Apocalypse, is frequently and very wrongly referred to as a 'mystic' scripture whereas it is in fact, unlike Liber AL, very exact.[70] Taking the Apocalypse of St. John as the true guide—though it is not by any means the only one as the doctrine of Cosmic Cycles exists in all authentic traditions—it becomes clear we have arrived at the time figured there by the opening of the sixth seal. It remains for the seventh to be opened, which is the closure of time for the present race of humanity:[71]

> And I saw another mighty angel come down from heaven, clothed with a cloud: and a rainbow was upon his head, and his face was as it were the sun, and his feet as pillars of fire:
>
> And the angel which I saw stand upon the sea and upon the earth lifted up his hand to heaven,
>
> And sware by him that liveth for ever and ever, who created heaven, and the things that therein are, and the earth, and the things that therein are, and the sea, and the things which are therein, that there should be time no longer:
>
> But in the days of the voice of the seventh angel, when he shall begin to sound, the mystery of God should be finished, as he hath declared to his servants the prophets.

---

[70] Some persons, perhaps enthralled by the 'Beast' Crowley, have sought to compare Liber AL vel Legis with the book of Revelation, which is really quite absurd: the latter is precisely structured and conforms with all other traditional knowledge, such as the Vedas, while the former is fragmentary and adulterated with the personal thoughts and ambitions of the writer.

[71] From Revelation 10: 1 and 10: 5–7.

The Sphinx: Time and Alchemy

The Sphinx may be regarded as an astronomical clock. Its position on the plateau of Giza is precisely aligned with the point on the horizon where the sun rises at the spring equinox. This point is used as a reference to calculate the astronomical cycle known as the precession of the equinoxes—the name given to the progression of the spring or vernal equinoctial point through the constellations of the Zodiac. The full cycle extends approximately 26,000 years and thus can be said to comprise twelve astrological ages a little more than 2,000 years each.[72] There is need to first dispell some erroneous notions that have arisen. Since Darwin's theories were adopted by modern science, the occultists arising out of the nineteenth century and onward have tried to explain traditional knowledge by making it fit 'evolution', and so have translated human experience over time into 'improvement', matching another favourite popular scientific term, 'progress'. In fact, the reverse is true when we regard the development of man over the great ages of time. As previously mentioned, the 'shape' of the Cosmic Cycles is circular, or more exactly, spiralic, as nothing ever returns exactly the same once it has reached the end of its cycle. At the beginning of a Manvantara of four great Yugas the world is very close to the principle. The primordial tradition is at one with the supreme principle of reality, to which all else is merely contingent. As we move through time—which is particular to the human state of being as in reality manifestation is simultaneous—we move further and further away from spiritual reality. While consciousness does not change, for it depends on a supra-human source, the mind of man degrades over time as it is further (spatially) from the true principles that govern existence. The fourth and last Age of Kali Yuga is naturally an Age of Darkness; man is for the most part ignorant of spiritual realities.

To accommodate this fall into ignorance, the primordial tradition adopts new forms, appropriate to the mentality of men, so there is still a chance of them knowing reality. All this is ordained by the Lord of the Manvantara (Sanskrit Ishvara) and his Shakti power, which as we have also explained, has nothing to do with any human being. Thus when the ancient Egyptian civilisation withdrew completely, its language forgotten, the seeds of Hermeticism and alchemy were cast out all over the world, resulting in many strange new blooms.

---

[72] For the history of the Sphinx, see Appendices, 'Restoration of the Sphinx'.

The Sphinx, seen as an astronomical clock, points to the cyclical nature of the life of the universe. An entire Manvantara consisting of four Yugas spans approximately 64,000 years, five Great Years, although over such a duration, time itself undergoes change, for time is qualitative, not quantitative in reality.[73] The cycle passes through four stages:[74]

1. The Golden Age where man is closest to spiritual reality.

2. The Silver Age, where is the first admixture of necessity and adaptive means but for the most part truth prevails.

3. The Bronze Age. By the mid-point it could be said that 'good' and 'evil' come about in the world. This could be symbolised by a circle with one hemisphere white and the other black.[75] By the end of this great era there is a need for kings and warriors to uphold truth to preserve equilibrium. There is thus peace and justice.

4. The Age of Iron. In the Kali Yuga the need for initiation arises. Previous to that, truth was perceptible to all without the need for special practices, yoga and so forth. The use of magick comes about and sometimes it becomes 'black magic', when the supreme principle is either knowingly denied or simply absent by ignorance. Towards the end of the Kali Yuga nearly all magick is black, in this way. Man loses sight of all spiritual reality and constructs counterfeits of initiation, such as psychological analysis. Finally there is death and dissolution of this world at the end of time. The return to eternity comes about in an 'instant', as does the Golden Age of a new Cosmic Cycle, but there is no return to the previous state.

It is necessary to dispel one of the countless delusions that have arisen as we draw near the end of the current Great Year and an entire Manvantara. It has been put about, sometimes with political intentions, that the Golden Age is in the 'future', and will come about on earth, for the present race of humans. This is totally false as the Golden Age is preceded by the ending of this world.

---

[73] Each Manu (Lord or Ishvara) reigns over a Manvantara. A total of 14 Manus reign successively in one Kalpa (day of Brahma). It is impossible to be exact when putting dates to these; the ancients used symbolic numbers.
[74] The Bronze and Iron Ages are not those of historians. There might be some overlap but there is no exact correspondence.
[75] There is a spatial relationship between cycles. The Yugas are not equal in terms of time so that the Golden Age is much longer than all the others, and the last Age of Darkness is comparatively (and thankfully) short-lived.

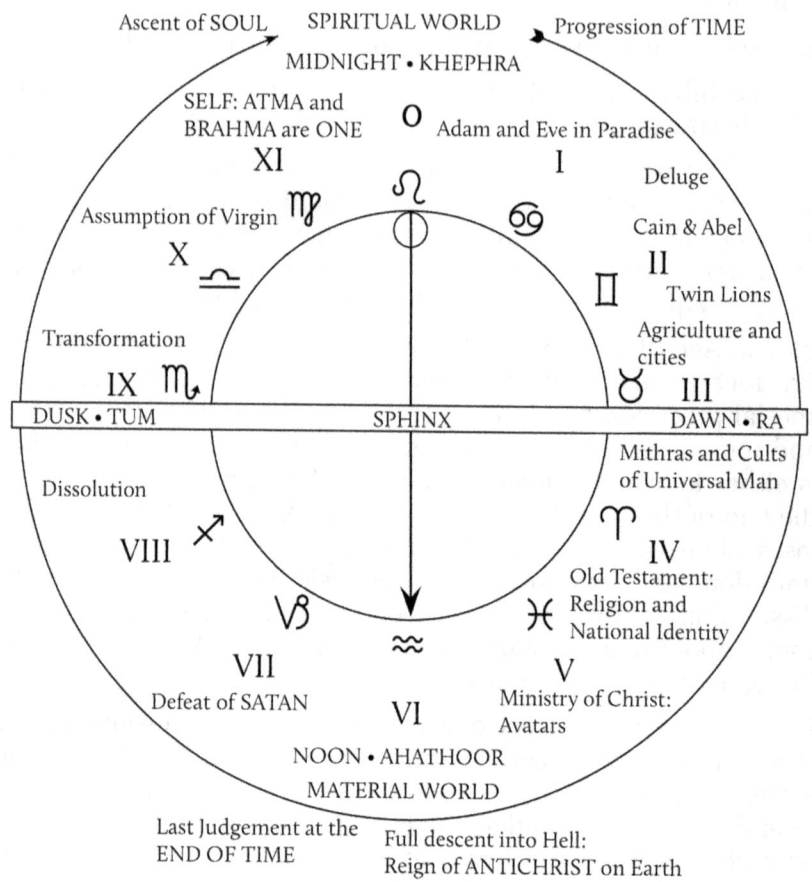

The Sphinx: Cycle of Descent and Ascent

What we are really concerned with here is the last Great Year, that commenced with Leo the Lion and ends with Aquarius, and that is the completion of a Manvantara. It is needful to understand that as there are four great Yugas, there also 'worlds within worlds', or lesser cycles. The precessional cycles are one such lesser cycle. Over the six precessional Zodiac signs of this last Great Year are formed micro-ages lasting for a little over 2,000 years each. These, as with a Great Year, mirror to a certain extent the gradual fall into darkness that is seen over the Yugas. The precession tracks backwards through the regular order of the Zodiac signs. The first Zodiacal Age in the Great Year was Leo, corresponding to the Sphinx herself. The one that immediately followed it was the Age of Cancer, then Gemini, then Taurus. Finally Aries, which reached its end around the time of the reign of Alexander in Egypt, then Pisces, which was the advent of Christianity in the West, while in India the *Yoga-Sutras* were written down by sages to preserve the knowledge. We are now at the cusp of the Age of Aquarius, which ends the Kali Yuga.[76]

The Zodiac with its four Kerubic or 'fixed' signs—Taurus, Leo, Scorpio and Aquarius—is one of the images of the metamorphic life cycle. The Sphinx stands at the heart of the twelve signs of the Zodiac and the Kerubic signs are her four aspects. The macrocosmic cycle was referred to as the Great Year by the Greeks and Persians, based on the precession of the equinoxes. The number twelve also forms the basis of the Sphinx's microcosmic counterpart, the human soul. The microcosmic cycle of the soul was described by the ancient Egyptians as having twelve hours.[77]

Using the symbol of the precessional clock of twelve signs and twelve hours, the cycle begins at hour zero which is also the twelfth hour. This is the hour of the androgyne, figured by Adam Kadmon in the Hebraic tradition, Hoor-paar-kraat in the Egyptian, and Universal Man in the Arabic. It is the hour of bliss where Adam and Eve dwell in perfect harmony in the Garden of Eden and are not separate beings. It is the Primordial State par excellence. This naturally mirrors the dawning of the Golden Age at the very beginning of the Manvantara, thousands of years ago in terms of terrestrial time.

---

[76] For historical detail, see the 'Chronological Table', Appendices.
[77] The ancient Egyptians used a system by which twelve hours were attributed to the day and twelve hours to the night, indicating the dual nature of the cycle that takes place in the visible as well as in the invisible world.

The first hour symbolises being born into a material existence, as figured by Cancer (♋), the sign of the Mother in all traditions. In terms of history, the Age of Cancer also coincides with a great deluge, very likely the same that is recorded in the biblical tale of Noah's Ark and in which the famed Atlantis, as centre or seat of the primordial tradition, was sunk, or otherwise disappeared. This is not to be confused with the great deluge that occurred at the very beginning of the Manvantara, but there is naturally an echoing of this at the beginning of a Great Year. The symbol for Cancer, the fourth sign in the zodiacal order, is strikingly similar to the Chinese *yin-yang*. It will be useful to repeat what was said earlier in this regard:[78]

> To use the Taoist terminology, the sage must become *yin* to the *yang* of the primordial principle, so that earth and heaven may be reunited. The soul is able to 'give birth to herself', or in other terms, accomplish the miracle of resurrection. It is the rôle and function of Isis to give life, for she is life itself, and the breath of life, the *ankh*, seat, throne or foundation of all that can exist.

This adumbrates what is figured on the other side of the wheel of the Sphinx at the eleventh hour, and the Assumption of the Virgin Mary. The name 'Mary' is derived from 'sea', in this case the great sea that transcends time and space, the 'heaven' of Nuit. Thus what is done outwardly in time, from the first to the sixth hour, is done inwardly on the Soul's Journey or ascent of the worlds from the sixth to the twelfth hours. As the Virgin, or Hermit of Tarot, the soul is Mary, the bride of Christ or Logos assimilated into the body of Nuit. The Scarlet Woman thus 'achieves Hadit' (III: 45).

The immersion of the soul in the waters of life at the beginning of the cycle is symbolised in the Gospel by the rituals of St. John the Baptist. The latter was born six months before Jesus; their respective births therefore coincide with the summer and winter solstices. The summer solstice takes place in the sign of Cancer, ruled by the Moon. The Sun (Heaven) is therefore said to be in the house of his Mother (Earth). The baptism conferred by John upon Jesus prepared and purified the latter for his ministry, which was to initiate his disciples through a baptism or birth into spirit. In the Gospel, the baptism is called the *second birth*—a birth not of the flesh but of the spirit, through which the soul realises her identity with the divine Word. As emphatically put in the book of John, 3: 3–8:

---

[78] See 'The Beast and Leviathan'.

> Verily, verily, I say unto thee, Except a man be born again, he cannot see the kingdom of God. Nicodemus saith unto him, How can a man be born when he is old? Can he enter the second time into his mother's womb, and be born? Jesus answered, Verily, verily, I say unto thee, Except a man be born of water and of the spirit, he cannot enter into the kingdom of God. That which is born of the flesh is flesh; and that which is born of the spirit is spirit. Marvel not that I said unto thee, Ye must be born again. The wind bloweth where it listeth, and thou hearest the sound thereof, but canst not tell whence it cometh, and whither it goeth: so is every one that is born of the spirit.

The second hour is figured by Gemini, the Twins of the Zodiac. This is aptly corresponded to alchemical *separatio*. Wherever there is antagonism or disequilibrium, order must be restored, through an initial separation then reuniting of elements in a new form. This has a justice aspect, to bring peace, mirrored on the other side of the clock by the Scales of Libra or the Egyptian Ma'at. It is therefore also a weighing of the heart. As a historical era, there are many examples of dual lions in Egypt and Assyria. The *aker* lions of Egypt probably owe to this time, the two beasts symbolising the entrance to and from the underworld, also figured by the equinoxes.

The biblical tale of Cain and Abel aptly symbolises the need for the reconciliation of a dualistic opposition in the soul. The name of 'Cain' (קין) has the root meaning of contraction or centralised force, and is literally associated with a lance, spear or weapon. It is also linked through its common root with the reed, which the Egyptians used to mark out time by the cutting of notches. Cain was the brother of Abel and firstborn son of Adam and Eve.[79] The name of Abel on the other hand has the meaning of 'space' (הבל). The tale of Cain and Abel in Genesis may therefore be construed cosmologically. Abel is 'space', circulation (heart) and so the type of the nomad or wanderer, whereas Cain is the farmer that will eventually build great cities founded on agriculture. Cain is 'time', which is why he was born of Eve first, before Abel, 'space'. Time is perceived before space is known. Thought does not occupy space but objects of perception fill space, and can be measured.

---

[79] Cain first appears in the biblical book of Genesis, 4: 1.

Notably, the first city built by Cain was named Enoch (חנוך), which has the meaning of 'Initiation'—initiation was not needed until agriculture predominated and men were bound to one location and could (therefore) build libraries and temples. In order to preserve the primordial tradition, and so that men would not forget God altogether, 'centres' were established, which are not only physical constructions but subtle or psychic plane repositories. The killing of the nomadic Abel by Cain prophesied that eventually it would be impossible to lead a nomadic existence and that all would be more or less forced to occupy cities and be counted, registered, recorded and made subject to state laws designed to be equally applicable to all persons under every circumstance. Once the true centres are lost or abandoned, cities become the abodes of the Qliphoth or shells of dead things. There is a further implication, which was written about by René Guénon, where at the end of the Manvantara, of which the final phase is the Age of Kali Yuga (the present time), there is no longer any space.[80] As soon as space runs out completely, time ceases and all is withdrawn into the *mahapralaya*, the great dissolution.

Thus by the end of the second hour there comes the real need for initiation to preserve the principial knowledge in the Age of Kali Yuga, which coincides with the third hour and sign of the Bull. Notably, most ancient Zodiacs begin with the Bull, not the Ram, which came about towards the end of the precessional Age of Aries. In the third hour we have the cults of Universal Man, such as Mithras, which is a preservation of the divine androgyne figured at the very beginning of this cycle. It should be here mentioned that the Gods such as Mithras, known in India, Persia and the mediterranean were symbolised at the centre of a wheel or 'celestial egg' of cosmos, but the Gods do not symbolise cosmos. They are the principle of Pure Being by which the cosmological sphere is able to come about. On the other side of the clock, Taurus is mirrored by Scorpio, which includes the transformation or ascent of the soul to an entirely new state of being, beyond form altogether, which ultimately means transcending the human state and passing beyond time forever. In Egypt, the precessional Age of Taurus marked the first dynastic kings, later called pharaohs. At the beginning their identities are hard to trace, because they were identified with the Manu (Sanskrit) or Menes (Egyptian), the Lord of the Manvantara as 'Legislator' and Logos.[81]

---

[80] *The Reign of Quantity and the Signs of the Times* [Sophia Perennis].
[81] Cf. 'King Scorpion and the Royal Way', *Nu Hermetica*.

It follows then that in the fourth hour of the soul, which equates to the precessional Age of Aries, comes the early formation of religions, which simultanously was to accomodate emerging nation states and to meet the need for national identity. Thus we have the Patriarchs of the Old Testament and in Egypt the ascendancy of the solar principle in the form of a Ram, typified by Amoun Ra. In this time the centre of all operations in Egypt was Waset, 'The Place of Ordinance', known to the Greeks as Thebes. This coincides with the time of our *Stele of Revealing* and the cult of Ankh-af-na-khonsu. In fact, Egypt resisted the attempts of the profane ruler Akhenaten to establish something like a religion, and his regime was fated not to last very long in terms of Egyptian dynasties. In terms of alchemy this period relates to the special fire of *ascesis* or *tapas*, which comes about when necessary austerities are practiced within a discipline. This is aptly mirrored on the other side of the clock by Sagittarius and the fire that brings dissolution of the 'body of the king' so that the ultimate transformation is possible:

> *If the body of the King dissolve, he shall remain in pure ecstasy for ever. Nuit! Hadit! Ra-Hoor-Khuit! The Sun, Strength and Sight, Light; these are for the servants of the Star and the Snake.*[82]

Early Christianity began in Hellenic Egypt, not Palestine. The fifth hour and precessional Age of Pisces heralds the ministry of Christ Jesus, whose work is to preserve the primordial tradition through rites of initiation, commencing with baptism, typifying the mutable waters of the sign of the Fishes. The fish was also an early symbol for Christ, as was the Egyptian Ankh, which was later transmuted into the crucifix. Christianity has a rather obscure beginning, perhaps typical of the relatively advanced degradation of the Age of Kali Yuga. The earliest forms of Christianity, not even called 'Christian', were clearly initiatic but as this was developed into a religion the rites were sublimated into exoteric church procedures. Thus eventually, baptism was no longer an initiatic rite but something that was even conferred on new born babes—who, as Guénon has noted, can hardly be said to be prepared for initiation![83] Along with religion and its theological interpretations came the danger of Dualism, especially in those religions which tend to anthropomorphise God. The demiurgic aspect of God, really an inversion, inevitably leads to objectification.

---

[82] II: 21.
[83] René Guénon, *Christian Esoterism* [Sophia Perennis].

Thus mirroring the fifth hour on the other side of the clock we have the seventh hour and the sign of Capricorn, typified by Satan as Adversary. From hereon Satan will take on many forms, ultimately the Antichrist, which is the anti-spiritual force in man that has reached its apparent or illusionary triumph at the present time. It is an illusionary triumph because it does not partake of any real or true principle but on its own *sub-infra* plane it is of course a devastating force.

The sixth hour is the exact midpoint of the cycle, and corresponds to the present time, on the cusp of the Age of Aquarius. Here we have the apparent triumph of the anti-spiritual force, which according to tradition is short-lived. For the soul this then corresponds to the full descent into hell. Of course, in this time of great confusion only the Initiates will understand this and feel pain and suffering—which they must of course master. The masses of humanity will fall into a trance of almost total unknowing, duped by the hypnotic spells transmitted through media and digital technology, bemused and excited by every new invention of Antichrist. For the Initiates, and perhaps those who are still faithful to the religious symbolism, and that have resisted the tendency to place it as second to the illusions of modern sciences, the way is mirrored now by the zero hour where all this began. At the point of the great dissolution at the end of time, the soul must be prepared to confront all the darkness and fear of death not only in the world but within her own heart. In this time, atavisms arising from the *sub-infra* level, otherwise Qliphoth, are a real danger. Even Initiates to the level of the second birth are able to succumb to the sense of hopelessness and despair that the System of Antichrist promotes and encourages, not to mention a constant state of anxiety in a human world that is mutable and unstable, where everything is changed and updated with increasing rapidity. Laws are changed on a monthly or even weekly basis. It is important to realise then that Leo the Lion has a dual nature. On the one hand he is a symbol of Christ, as an avatar that leads the way to freedom, and on the other hand he is a symbol of Antichrist, counted as 666 in the book of Revelation.

Christ returns to judge the world at the End of Time and in the Book of the Law this is figured by Horus, of whom the Avenging Angel is one aspect. Either way the symbolism points to the return of the Scarlet Woman to indivisible unity and beyond even that; the damned simply cease to exist, having no real substance (Greek υλη).

The seventh hour is not within time, then, but symbolises the first stage of the Journey of the Soul on the ascent. The defeat of Satan figured here had to be anticipated by the soul's ability to see through the tricks of the System of Antichrist. Identity is not sought for in anything other than the true Self (Atma or Hadit in superior aspect). The dissolution of the eighth hour signifies death of the body and indeed the whole world of humanity; the risen soul does not perish however, but is transformed. The full measure of this comes at the ninth hour of Scorpio, when the 'body of the king' has fully dissolved.

The tenth hour is figured by Libra, the Scales of Ma'at. The soul or Scarlet Woman has already passed through death and dissolution, so this is no longer the trial of the Hall of Judgement but has more to do with Synesis, which is a lesser attribute of divine Sophia, the feminine wisdom symbol of Gnosticism and Shakti of the Tantras.[84] It is really the intellectual 'understanding' of the Intelligible, by 'putting things together', which still implies of course a certain dualism of the subject and object. It is thus also comparable to a lesser *samadhi*, to which Gnosis, 'direct knowledge' (Sanskrit *jnana*), is the superior. The Shakti or living Spirit is able to embrace both kinds of wisdom, the lesser and the greater, and this is how it is possible for the soul to become fully assumed as the Virgin Mary or the 'pure soul' in the eleventh hour. The Hermit or Virgin represents the soul freed from Leviathan and assumed into heaven by her magical child or star—as is symbolised not only in the Christian narrative but in scriptures of considerably greater antiquity. Here, she passes into immortality as a jewel in the heavenly body of Nuit. Shining as a diamond or star, her mutable substance has been fully united with the imperishable, the immortal, and beyond that is the possibility of the total liberation (*moksha*), in which the zero hour is regained and there is no further return to the manifest existence. She has passed into Eternity. Atma and Brahma, or Hadit and Nuit, are 'one and none'.

AUM

---

[84] See 'Gnosis of the Thirty Aeons', especially the diagram 'Realm of Sophia within the Gnostic Cosmograph', *Thunder Perfect Gnosis*.

The Holy Guardian Angel

The (Egyptian) Book of the Law makes no direct mention of any Holy Guardian Angel, but as the idea has become so very deeply embedded into the milieu surrounding the book and its writer, it will be helpful if we go some way in explaining what it really is.[85] Nearly all traditions include the idea that from the beginning of time God made two orders of creatures. These consisted of the spiritual order and the corporeal order—the angelic and the earthly. At the very centre of creation was placed the human creature that partakes of both orders, since he is composed of body and spirit. 'Angel' is the name of the office of the spiritual creatures. The name comes from the Greek word *angelos*, which means, 'a messenger'. The concept of an angel being sent by God with a special purpose is part of the Judaeo Christian tradition. There are references in both Old and New Testaments. According to the book of Exodus:

> Behold, I send an Angel before thee, to keep thee in the way, and to bring thee into the place which I have prepared. Beware of him, and obey his voice, provoke him not; for he will not pardon your transgressions: for my name is in him. But if thou shalt indeed obey his voice, and do all that I speak; then I will be an enemy unto thine enemies, and an adversary unto thine adversaries.[86]

This rather unforgiving angel typifies the spirit of the 'old books' of the Bible, but in the book of St. John an angel is sent by the Lord in the name of Christ, to keep the way until the end of time, as he is about to withdraw from the earth:[87]

> But the Comforter, which is the Holy Ghost, whom the Father will send in my name, he shall teach you all things, and bring all things to your remembrance, whatsoever I have said unto you.
> Peace I leave with you, my peace I give unto you: not as the world giveth, give I unto you. Let not your heart be troubled, neither let it be afraid.

---

[85] We have dealt with this subject quite exhaustively in previous works and cannot cover every aspect here. The reader is referred especially to *Way of Knowledge*, which includes six chapters discussing the topic from different angles. See pp. 45–78 in that volume.
[86] Exodus 23: 20–22.
[87] John 14: 26–30.

> Ye have heard how I said unto you, I go away, and come again unto you. If ye loved me, ye would rejoice, because I said, I go unto the Father: for my Father is greater than I.
>
> And now I have told you before it come to pass, that, when it is come to pass, ye might believe.
>
> Hereafter I will not talk much with you: for the prince of this world cometh, and hath nothing in me.

The 'prince of this world' refers to the coming of the Antichrist near the end of time. Therefore the angel is none other than the Holy Ghost or Holy Spirit, by which men can still receive the blessing of the Lord even in the darkest times on earth. It is of absolutely paramount significance, because if it were otherwise, how could the presence of Christ Jesus be with us in our hour of greatest need?

By nature, angels are spirits that are servants and messengers of God—those 'that excel in strength, that do his commandments, hearkening unto the voice of his word'.[88] As spiritual creatures, angels have intelligence and will. From infancy to death human life is surrounded by the intercession of the angels. According to St. Basil:

> Beside each man and woman stands an angel as shepherd leading them to life.

In the words of the Gospel of St. Matthew, 18: 10:

> Take heed that ye despise not one of these little ones; for I say unto you, that in heaven their angels do always behold the face of my Father which is in heaven.

This has been wrongly construed by sentimentalists as having to do with actual children or infants. In fact 'little ones' refers to those who are able, unlike the rich man in the parable, to pass through the eye of a needle. It refers then to a stage in the life of a *sannyasin*, as this is put in the terms of the Hindu tradition, where he has no desire for anything but to know God, and he therefore abides in simplicity.

According to scriptural writing, not everyone has such an angel to help them on the way, because some really belong to the Devil, whether this is a matter of will or not—it should also be considered that, contrary to some modern ideologies, man is not born 'equal', as nothing in nature can be the same. We all have unique and different possibilities. For the same reason, not everyone can be initiated.

---

[88] Psalms, 103: 20.

According to the testimony of St. John, 8: 44, these are the words of Christ Jesus to those who sought to kill him, and that claimed to be the sons of Abraham:

> Jesus said unto them, If God were your Father, ye would love me: for I proceeded forth and came from God; neither came I of myself, but he sent me.
>
> Why do ye not understand my speech? even because ye cannot hear my word.
>
> Ye are of your father the devil, and the lusts of your father ye will do. He was a murderer from the beginning, and abode not in the truth, because there is no truth in him. When he speaketh a lie, he speaketh of his own: for he is a liar, and the father of it.
>
> And because I tell you the truth, ye believe me not.[89]

In this context the Devil is the originator of the illusion of separation, and therefore of suffering and death, the condition of man after the fall. The Devil also has his (fallen) angels that are cast out into the earth when Christ returns to judge the world at the end of time:

> And the great dragon was cast out, that old serpent, called the Devil, and Satan, which deceiveth the whole world: he was cast out into the earth, and his angels were cast out with him.[90]

---

[89] In this narrative, Jesus addresses some Jews who pretend to follow him but are really plotting to kill him. They claim they are descended from Abraham, the father of their race, but Jesus rejects this notion and says their father is the devil. He barely escapes with his life, as they would have stoned him to death. What these passages clearly reveal is the difference between the teaching of Christ Jesus, which is obviously about direct knowledge of God, and those who merely follow scriptural law but are unregenerate. By reference to the 'murderer from the beginning', Jesus then identifies these conspirators with Cain, who murdered Abel in Genesis. Abel, as 'shepherd', is identified with the Egyptian tradition of Hermes. As Abel was killed and could not have descendants, scriptural law has it that the Lord gave Eve a third child, Seth—otherwise the primordial tradition would be lost with the death of Abel. Gnostics, sometimes called Sethians, have always insisted they are of the generation of Seth, not Cain. Therefore Jesus, contrary to what theologians have always denied, was a Gnostic.

[90] Revelation 12: 9.

In Liber AL vel Legis, the separation is not so much about that lie begotten by the devil, the father of lies since the beginning of time, but is more pertaining to the cosmological sphere. Manifestation is only possible through separation or duality. Thus it is necessary and vital since it is the very essence of creation, or existence:

> *For I am divided for love's sake, for the chance of union. This is the creation of the world, that the pain of division is as nothing, and the joy of dissolution all.*[91]

That statement does not in any way disagree with the teaching of Advaita Vedanta, or indeed of the *Yoga Sutras*. All pain and sorrow is contingent and only appears that way from the point of view of not knowing supreme reality. The Hermetic tradition also presupposes that the solution to suffering and death rests upon man's ability to obtain union with the Word of God. The natural soul inhabits a world that by its very nature is fallen, viz., in a state of separation from the eternal and real. To unite with the divine Word the soul requires the mediation of one capable of acting as a messenger between her world and eternity. The Word may then be born in the soul, after a manner of speaking. The soul is then born a second time, which is the birth into spirit spoken of previously.[92] The spiritual child begotten by the soul will assume her in his own wisdom and immortality, as in the testimony of John:

> I tell you most solemnly, unless a man is born through water and the spirit, he cannot enter the kingdom of God: what is born from the flesh is flesh; what is born from the spirit is spirit.[93]

If the soul should neglect the Great Work, then she and her 'child' may certainly suffer the fate of annihilation. A warning is delivered through the voice of Ra Hoor Khuit, the Angel of judgement and death:

> *Let the Scarlet Woman beware! If pity and compassion and tenderness visit her heart; if she leave my work to toy with old sweetnesses; then shall my vengeance be known. I will slay me her child: I will alienate her heart: I will cast her out from men: as a shrinking and despised harlot shall she crawl through dusk wet streets, and die cold and an-hungered.*[94]

---

[91] I: 29–30.
[92] See 'The Hermetic Great Work' and 'The Sphinx, Time and Alchemy'.
[93] John, 3: 5–6.
[94] III: 43.

In I: 41, the (Egyptian) Book of the Law curses the 'word of Sin', the errors and confusion that are piled up higher than the tower of Babel. There is indeed a Great Work to be done (*kriyayoga*, 'action'). This is only possible through a messenger or bridge between the worlds. It is integral to the doctrine of the Western Tradition that every human being born into this world has a counterpart in the invisible world. The implication conveyed through the remnants of the Hermetic tradition that have survived is that the presence of the Angel (or Daemon) is blotted out of consciousness by the rational mind. The 'child' that is born out of the soul crippled by reason is death. The spiritual impregnation or irradiation by initiatic transmission, if a valid source has been contacted, is then abortive; the soul cannot participate in the joy promised by Nuit to her chosen ones.

It will be seen at once then that the Will of Thelema cannot be confused with the quest for personal freedom and individual self-expression that characterises the ideals of 'the people'—and the advertising industry. The achievement of the soul depends on vital spiritual factors. Far from being a type of hedonism, as some would have it, Thelema requires the soul to apply ruthless discrimination on the path. This is made all the more difficult since only the knowledge of the True Will conveyed by the Holy Guardian Angel can provide the guiding truth for each soul—yet the spiritual work to be done has profound import to every man and every woman that is a star. The choice for the soul is still understood to be one of life on the one hand or annihilation on the other.

In the book of the prophet Ezekiel (41: 19), the inside of the Hekal or Hall of the Temple is described as being adorned with cherubs having two faces, the face of a man and the face of a lion. These represent the spiritual and the corporeal aspects of man as well as knowledge and power. The man or angel, and the lion, correspond to the zodiacal signs of Aquarius and Leo. It is the polarity ruling the present (and last) astronomical age. The union takes place in the second chamber of the Temple. The Initiate who passes through this chamber, that is, who unites with his Holy Guardian Angel, may attain to the knowledge symbolised by the third chamber of the Temple, the Holy of Holies.[95]

---

[95] The Temple described by Ezekiel has three parts, called the Ulam or Vestibule, the Hekal or Hall (the Holy), and the Debir or Sanctuary (the Holy of Holies). It is an almost exact replica of the Temple of Solomon described in Kings, I: 6.

In Liber AL vel Legis the spiritual counterpart of man is referred to by an Egyptian name, the Khabs. This has various meanings including 'worship', 'light', and 'star' (though the term is figurative and not usually referring to a star in the heavens). The star is latent until it emerges into the consciousness of the natural soul. Made conscious, it becomes the soul's aspiration to spiritual knowledge. The incarnation of the Word of the True Will within the Khabs fertilises it, so to speak. The Khabs is then able to manifest as a divine child whose body is called the Khu. The substance of the Khu body is extracted or distilled from the substance of the soul herself. Without the body provided by the natural soul the Khabs could not develop into a fully autonomous spiritual being. In other words the divine child grows out of the substance of the soul—not the soul out of the substance of the child. The spiritual child then ultimately assumes the entire substance of the soul as his own body. As Liber AL puts it:

The Khabs is in the Khu, not the Khu in the Khabs.[96]

The soul who then worships the Khabs, that is, who uplifts her mind in constant recollection of the higher source of knowledge (Sanskrit *boddhi*), receives the knowledge of Nuit:

Worship then the Khabs, and behold my light shed over you![97]

Note that the three words 'worship', 'light' and 'shed' (as in radiation of light or transmission) are all meanings of the one word Khabs. Such is the story of the incarnation of Jesus in the womb of Mary. The only difference is that religious doctrine insists this must be a one-time-only event whose operation depends entirely on historical authenticity. At the Egyptian centre of Aunnu (Heliopolis) thousands of years before the time of the historical Jesus, the birth of a god named Horus from the womb of a Virgin called Isis was celebrated. At Aunnu, Horus was uniquely revered as a double deity named Heru-Set.[98] By making analogy between spiritual regeneration and physical generation one would equate the following principles:

The Natural Soul is as the womb.
The Khabs is then as an egg in the womb.
The Word fertilising the egg is the spermatozoon.

---

[96] I: 8.
[97] I: 9.
[98] The biblical account of Christ's temptation by Satan continues the much earlier Egyptian narrative concerning the trials of Horus by Set.

This fertilisation of the egg thus doubles (or self-polarises) the egg. The Khu is the child's body that grows by receiving nourishment from his own mother, the soul. In the physical world the continuity of existence takes place through successive generations, each of which is subject to death. In the spiritual world the immortalisation of the mother-soul takes place through her child or star.

Aiwass does not speak on his own behalf. He is the hearer of the Word and the communicator of it to the soul. Through him, the voices of a trinity of Egyptian gods speak forth, revealing their mysteries. Aiwass holds the title of 'minister of Hoor-paar-kraat'.[99] He is the master of silence, in other words meditation: the silence in which the soul must enter to hear the Word, incarnate it and become it, to be within reach of the ultimate, which means passing into eternity. Aiwass is the messenger sent to reveal this sacred science:

> *Behold! it is revealed by Aiwass the minister of Hoor-paar-kraat. The Khabs is in the Khu, not the Khu in the Khabs.*[100]

The Khabs is known in the language of alchemy as the philosophers stone. In Greek, the word for 'stone', *psephos*, also means, 'a voice'. This is revealing of the relationship between the philosophers stone or Khabs and the Word, a relationship referred to in St. John's Revelation, II: 17. Here, Christ asks St. John to write to the angel of the church in Pergamos and say:[101]

> He that hath an ear, let him hear what the spirit saith unto the churches; To him that overcometh will I give to eat of the hidden manna, and will give him a white stone, and in the stone a new name written, which no man knoweth saving he that receiveth it.

Obtaining the 'Knowledge and Conversation of the Holy Guardian Angel' is the prerequisite to doing the Great Work. Without it, man is spiritually ignorant; his interaction with spirits is not in conformity with his True Will, but is directed by his Evil Genius to lead him to destruction. The Evil Genius is the root of separation from the love of Nuit, as she warns the practitioner in Liber AL, I: 52:

> *If the ritual be not ever unto me: then expect the direful judgements of Ra-Hoor-Khuit!*

---

[99] I: 7.
[100] I: 7–8.
[101] Pergamos means 'height' or 'elevation'.

The Last Judgement

Human consciousness inhabits a world ruled by finality. Man's knowledge of the eternal, where beginning and end are realised as simultaneous, unfolds between the marks of the beginning and the end of time. The initiation of the soul in time is punctuated by the events that prepare her for a final confrontation with truth and reality. The soul that wants to know God above all else undergoes transformation. This brings the possibilities of immortality and even ultimate liberation (Sanskrit *moksha*). Divided from spiritual reality through self-will, she loses substance and perishes. All spiritual traditions identify such a confrontation—be it called the Last Judgement, the Day of the Lord or simply 'death'—as the ultimate trial of the soul at the crossroads of initiation, as declared in III: 22:

> *I am the visible object of worship; the others are secret; for the Beast and his Bride are they: and for the winners of the Ordeal x.*

Liber AL vel Legis is a book of the dead in so far as the mystery it reveals is that of the ultimate ordeal. It is also a book of life. The key of life is the relationship of the soul with the Holy Guardian Angel—by which she may emerge triumphant from Ordeal x. Eschatological writings are found throughout the books of the Bible, particularly among the books of the prophets. They are also found in sections of the discourses of Christ Jesus recorded in the Gospels, in various Epistles of the New Testament and in St. John's Revelation. A consistent pattern runs throughout. The scriptures describe the soul's confrontation with evil that tests her spiritual integrity, fortifies her, cleanses her from sin or error and prepares her for salvation or, by upward transposition, eternal life. The confrontation with death includes the experience named 'the abomination of desolation' by the prophet Daniel and Jesus.[102] The eschatological discourse recorded in the Gospel of St. Matthew describes this great tribulation as a time when the deceptions of the world—called Maya, the weaver of the 'world illusion' in the East—will tempt the soul.[103] She is thus led away from the Word and the possibility of redemption. The soul capable of overcoming these deceptions will be redeemed by her faith in the Word, who will gather her elements into his own spiritual life.

---

[102] Daniel 9: 27 and Matthew 24: 15.
[103] Matthew 24: 1–31.

Understood in alchemical terms, the abomination of desolation is a descent into hell through which the soul is to encounter, consume and transmute the elements of her own being; she is then able to raise herself triumphant in a regenerated, immortal body or Khu. The elements that she is to assimilate in her descent into Hades will destroy her if she is cut off from the Holy Guardian Angel (and therefore her True Will). Putting that another way, she may fall prey to the seduction of sensory illusions (or 'false prophets'). Ra Hoor Khuit, the third person of the Thelemic Trinity, directly relates the Book of the Law to this ordeal. Concerning the funeral stone or stele of the cult Initiate named after the prophet Ankh-af-na-khonsu, Ra Hoor Khuit informs us:

That stélé they shall call the Abomination of Desolation...[104]

The first biblical reference to the abomination of desolation is recorded in the twelfth chapter of the book of Daniel. The book of Daniel is the last and most direct expression of messianic prophecy in the Old Testament.[105] The book of Daniel bears many similarities to the book of Ezekiel. Ezekiel and Daniel were both contemporaries of Ankh-af-na-khonsu, of the *Stele of Revealing*. They were prophets of the end of an age, heralding a crossing over into a new and darker age for humanity.[106] They asserted the doctrine of the angels. With its 'sealed book', its message for generations to come and its deliberately enigmatic style, the book of Daniel is closely related to that of Revelation.[107] In the latter, the seals of the closed books are broken and its words are secret no longer.[108] This is because the coming of the Lord is expected and 'the time is at hand'.[109]

---

[104] III: 19.

[105] The book of Daniel was probably completed in its present form at the end of the persecution—so-called—said to have taken place between 167 and 164 BC.

[106] The book of Daniel begins with a description of events said to take place at the time of the Babylonian King Nebuchadnezzar.

[107] Daniel 12: 4.

[108] Revelation 5–6.

[109] Revelation 22: 10.

The mysteries of the Last Judgement expounded in Liber AL vel Legis bear close comparison with the books of Daniel and Revelation. A study of the twelfth chapter of the Book of Daniel is thus helpful so we can understand the relationship between Daniel's 'abomination of desolation' and the funeral stele of an Ankh-af-na-khonsu priest in Thebes:

1. And at that time shall Michael stand up, the great prince which standeth for the children of thy people: and there shall be a time of trouble, such as never was since there was a nation even to that same time: and at that time thy people shall be delivered, every one that shall be found written in the book.

2. And many of them that sleep in the dust of the earth shall awake, some to everlasting life, and some to shame and everlasting contempt.

3. And they that be wise shall shine as the brightness of the firmament; and they that turn many to righteousness as the stars forever and ever.

4. But thou, O Daniel, shut up the words, and seal the book, even to the time of the end: many shall run to and fro, and knowledge shall be increased.

5. Then I Daniel looked, and, behold, there stood other two, the one on this side of the bank of the river, and the other on that side of the bank of the river.

6. And one said to the man clothed in linen, which was upon the waters of the river, How long shall it be to the end of these wonders?

7. And I heard the man clothed in linen, which was upon the waters of the river, when he held up his right hand and his left hand unto heaven, and sware by him that liveth for ever that it shall be for a time, two times, and an half; and when he shall have accomplished to scatter the power of the holy people, all these things shall be finished.

8. And I heard, but I understood not: then said I, O my Lord, what shall be the end of these things?

9. And he said, Go thy way, Daniel: for the words are closed up and sealed till the time of the end.

10. Many shall be purified, and made white, and tried; but the wicked shall do wickedly: and none of the wicked shall understand; but the wise shall understand.

11. And from the time that the daily sacrifice shall be taken away, and the abomination that maketh desolate set up, there shall be a thousand two hundred and ninety days.[110]

12. Blessed is he that waiteth, and cometh to the thousand three hundred and five and thirty days.[111]

13. But go thou thy way till the end be: for thou shalt rest, and stand in thy lot at the end of the days.

Verse 2 (above) is one of the key texts of the Old Testament on the resurrection of the body. The resurrected body is the Khu spoken of in Liber AL vel Legis, the light by which the Initiate may pass into the company of heaven at the end of time.

Verse 3 refers to 'the vault of heaven', body of Nuit or company of heaven, and the transformation of the Initiates who will be 'as bright as stars for all eternity'. In verse 4, Daniel is told that he 'must keep these words secret and the book sealed until the time of the End'. It was only at the 'time of the End' when the seal would be opened. As declared in Liber AL, II: 2:

> *Come! all ye, and learn the secret that hath not yet been revealed.*

The opening of the sealed book is central to the Revelation of St. John in which the Lamb of God (Christ) breaks open the seven seals.[112] There, as in Liber AL, the word 'come' or 'be with us' is uttered as the seals of knowledge are opened. 'Come' is Hadit's invitation to pass into the company of heaven as well as an expression of Nuit's love chant, 'To me! To me!'[113] 'God be-with-us' is also the name given to Jesus in the book of Matthew, I: 23:

> Behold, a virgin shall be with child, and shall bring forth a son, and they shall call his name Emmanuel, which being interpreted is, God with us.[114]

---

[110] 1,290 is expressed by the Hebrew letters Aleph, Resh, Tzaddi—or, ARTz (291), 'Earth'.
[111] 1,335 is written Aleph, Shin, Lamed, Hé—or, ShALH (336) 'attack, request or petition'.
[112] Revelation 6.
[113] Liber AL vel Legis I: 65.
[114] This verse recollects what is said in the book of Isaiah 7: 14 and 8: 8.

In verse 6, Daniel then asks: 'How long shall it be until the end of these wonders?' The answer is: 'it shall be for a time, two times, and an half'. Three and a half is the number of coils of the two serpents entwined around the Staff of Hermes. 'Three and a fraction' is also an expression of *Pi*, the ratio between the circle and the diameter, also expressive of an indefinite number as the fraction does not resolve. The ancients used symbolic numbers to calculate the Cosmic Cycles, and the use of *Pi* is notable in certain figures used in Hinduism. Thus any question concerning the end of time must involve *Pi*.

It is the Beast who carries the Scarlet Woman to her doom, the doom of Ordeal x also described in Revelation 18: 10:

> Alas, alas, that great city Babylon, that mighty city! for in one hour is thy judgment come.

This is echoed in Liber AL, I: 61, where Nuit declares:

> *For one kiss wilt thou then be willing to give all; but whoso gives one particle of dust shall lose all in that hour.*

The Scarlet Woman in this context is the natural soul, the material universe that will be destroyed at the end of time when objective and subjective states of consciousness are no longer separate. After her fall or Ordeal x, she is the heavenly Jerusalem seen by St. John and described in Revelation, 21: 1–5:

> And I saw a new heaven and a new earth: for the first heaven and the first earth were passed away; and there was no more sea.
> And I John saw the holy city, New Jerusalem, coming down from God out of heaven, prepared as a bride adorned for her husband.
> And I heard a great voice out of heaven saying, Behold, the tabernacle of God is with men, and he will dwell with them, and they shall be his people, and God himself shall be with them, and be their God.
> And God shall wipe away all tears from their eyes; and there shall be no more death, neither sorrow, nor crying, neither shall there be any more pain: for the former things are passed away.
> And he that sat upon the throne said, Behold, I make all things new. And he said unto me, Write: for these words are true and faithful.

The new heaven and new earth are the company of heaven promised by Nuit to her chosen in Liber AL, I: 53:

> *This shall regenerate the world, the little world my sister, my heart and my tongue, unto whom I send this kiss.*

The transformation of the Scarlet Woman—comparable to the body or host broken and eaten at a Mass—is described in the Acts of the Apostles where Peter receives a vision revealing that the soul must consume that which is impure so as to become an incorruptible vessel—an instruction often echoed in the Hindu Tantras:[115]

> Peter went up upon the housetop to pray about the sixth hour:
> And he became very hungry, and would have eaten: but while they made ready, he fell into a trance,
> And saw heaven opened, and a certain vessel descending unto him, as it had been a great sheet knit at the four corners, and let down to the earth:
> Wherein were all manner of four-footed beasts of the earth, and wild beasts, and creeping things, and fowls of the air.
> And there came a voice to him, Rise, Peter; kill, and eat.
> But Peter said, Not so, Lord; for I have never eaten any thing that is common or unclean.
> And the voice spake unto him again the second time, What God hath cleansed, that call not thou common.
> This was done thrice: and the vessel was received up again into heaven.

The transmutation of the flesh or Scarlet Woman into a spiritual body or Khu at the end of time is also described in Ezekiel where the prophet, in a vision, is led by an angel to the gate of the Temple of Jerusalem, the 'heavenly Jerusalem' later described by St. John in Revelation.

> Afterward he brought me again unto the door of the house; and, behold, waters issued out from under the threshold of the house eastward: for the forefront of the house stood toward the east, and the waters came down from under from the right side of the house, at the south side of the altar. Then brought he me out of the way of the gate northward, and led me about the way without unto the utter gate by the way that looketh eastward; and, behold, there ran out waters on the right side.[116]

The prophet is led through ever-deepening waters until they are so deep he can no longer cross them. The measurer of the line or Word then tells him that these are veritably the waters of life proceeding to the east, to the desert, and into the sea, and that as even the sea thereby shall be healed, so shall any creature that is touched by the waters of life.

---

[115] Acts 10: 9–16.
[116] Ezekiel 47: 1–2.

Fishermen shall then stand upon the water and cast their nets, catching as many kinds of fish as according to the kind of the fishermen. However:

> But the miry places thereof and the marshes thereof shall not be healed; they shall be given to salt. And by the river upon the bank thereof, on this side and on that side, shall grow all trees for meat, whose leaf shall not fade, neither shall the fruit thereof be consumed: it shall bring forth new fruit according to his months, because their waters they issued out of the sanctuary: and the fruit thereof shall be for meat, and the leaf thereof for medicine.[117]

The Temple described by Ezekiel is the body of the Adept stretched upon the cross of the four elements (North, South, East, West) and passing through the waters of time and space to the Last Judgement or precessional Age of Aquarius. The torrents of water described earlier are the waters of life or spiritual transmission pouring out from the world centre or terrestrial Eden. The waters grow wider and deeper, broadening throughout space represented by the sea. The fishermen are the souls of all those who are receptive to such transmission of the Word. The fishes and creeping things are the corruptible elements to be transformed by it. Those who do not, or are not able to 'abide in this bliss', as it is put in Liber AL, are therefore turned into 'sterile salt-pits', which is to say they are bereft of the waters of life.[118] They are caught in the trap of words alone, as scripture, science or the law of man's reason—static and cursed to atrophy. Ezekiel reveals that the cross, crossing point or abomination of desolation is the means by which the eternal draws manifestation back to itself. The cross or Tau is the symbol of Saturn or Time. The winning of Ordeal x gives consummate meaning to all man's dealings with angels, gods or other supernatural beings:

> *For I am divided for love's sake, for the chance of union. This is the creation of the world, that the pain of division is as nothing, and the joy of dissolution all.*[119]

According to Ra Hoor Khuit, Lord of the Last Judgement:

---

[117] Ezekiel 47: 11–12.
[118] Liber AL vel Legi, III: 39.
[119] Liber AL vel Legis I: 29–30.

> *I am the Lord of the Double Wand of Power; the wand of the force of Coph Nia—but my left hand is empty, for I have crushed an Universe; and nought remains...*
>
> *There is a splendour in my name hidden and glorious, as the sun of midnight is ever the son. The ending of the words is the Word Abrahadabra.*[120]

Abrahadabra is the 'reward of Ra Hoor Khut'.[121] It is worth noting that the word, which was a contrivance of Crowley's from some years previous to the writing of Liber AL vel Legis, adds (intentionally) to the number 418. This is Qabalistically equal to ChTATh, which has the meaning of error, mistake, sin or transgression, a slip (or fall) or misfortune—though also 'atonement'. The number 418 is also that of 'Fountain of the living'.[122]

It is, on the one hand, the incorruptible body granted to the soul who has been justified at the hour of Judgement, as according to the Egyptian tradition.[123] On the other hand it spells doom for the soul who refuses, or is simply unable, to choose wisely.

The ordeal of the abomination of desolation is the prerequisite of what Judaism calls the Passover—the passing over from one world to the next. It was at the Jewish festival of the Passover—the celebration of the supposed crossing of the Red Sea lead by Moses—that Judas betrayed Christ. There followed the passion, crucifixion and resurrection; that is, the ordeal and passing over of Christ Jesus (or Emmanuel). The celebration of the final Passover meal between Christ Jesus and his disciples became known as the Last Supper, and marked the institution of the Eucharist or Christian Mass. In the Gospel of St. Luke, the following details are recorded concerning the preparations of the Last Supper:

---

[120] Liber AL vel Legis III: 72 and III: 74–75.
[121] III: 1.
[122] MQIR ChIIM = 418.
[123] The heart is balanced in the scales of Ma'at when the word is perfectly expressed or uttered. See E. A. Wallis Budge, *The Gods of the Egyptians*, Volume 1, Chapter XIII, 'Thoth and Maat'.

> Then came the day of unleavened bread, when the passover must be killed. And he sent Peter and John, saying, Go and prepare us the passover, that we may eat. And they said unto him, Where wilt thou that we prepare? And he said unto them, Behold, when ye are entered into the city, there shall a man meet you, bearing a pitcher of water; follow him into the house where he entereth in. And ye shall say unto the good man of the house, The Master saith unto thee, Where is the guest-chamber, where I shall eat the passover with my disciples? And he shall shew you a large upper room furnished: there make ready. And they went, and found as he had said unto them: and they made ready the passover.[124]

The Last Supper will be eaten in a house to which a man, 'bearing a pitcher of water', will lead the disciples. The man in question refers to the astrological glyph for the Age of Aquarius. This happens to coincide with the image of Hrumachis or Hormaku as Sphinx.[125] On the Hermetic Tree of Life, the path of Aquarius extends from Tiphereth to Chokmah and crosses the Abyss of Da'ath—the crossing, Passover, or 'place of no return'. Liber AL vel Legis thus conveys the spiritual law of the Last Judgement. The soul that has passed through the Ordeal x by the power of Ra Hoor Khuit has thereby 'achieved Hadit'. The transformation of the forces of evil and death undergone by the soul is addressed thus:

> *But let her raise herself in pride! Let her follow me in my way! Let her work the work of wickedness! Let her kill her heart! Let her be loud and adulterous! Let her be covered with jewels, and rich garments, and let her be shameless before all men! Then will I lift her to pinnacles of power: then will I breed from her a child mightier than all the kings of the earth. I will fill her with joy: with my force shall she see and strike at the worship of Nu: she shall achieve Hadit.*[126]

This verse has sometimes been interpreted as though it presented us with a literal feminine (or even feminist) rôle model. However, in the context of initiation, the soul's 'work of wickedness' is to have defeated the dogs (or gods) of human reason. She is 'loud' for she has uttered the Word of her True Will, thus exorcising the demonic forces that enthral humanity in its susceptibility to 'reasonable' manipulation.

---

[124] Luke 22: 7–13.
[125] See 'The Sphinx: Symbol of Love and Will'.
[126] III: 44–45.

Her 'adultery' consists of the willed betrayal of her marriage to all that binds the uninitiated to time and death, choosing instead to pursue her love of God. Hence her shamelessness before all men: the soul no longer fears the rejection or disapproval of the 'many and the known' who, under the spell of the dogs of reason, will fall under the direful judgment of Ra Hoor Khuit and become as sterile as salt-pits. The path—and its difficulty—is revealed.[127]

The orientalist Kenneth Grant studied the holograph manuscripts and diaries of Crowley while staying with him at his retirement home in Hastings. He testified to the likelihood that Crowley wrote down the three chapters of Liber AL vel Legis on the 1st, 2nd and 3rd April 1904, which coincided with the three days of Easter that year—as opposed to the 8th, 9th and 10th as Crowley later claimed. The coincidence between the reception of Liber AL and the three days of Easter that are rooted in the tradition of the Passover is supported by the words of Ra Hoor Khuit, who tells the prophet

That stélé they shall call the Abomination of Desolation.[128]

The soul who has realised Nuit has realised her self as conterminous with all worlds, her Integral Self. She therefore partakes in the joy of the world as opposed to the deceptive comforts and weak desires of the 'slaves of Because'. In II: 21, Hadit declares:

We have nothing with the outcast and the unfit: let them die in their misery. For they feel not. Compassion is the vice of kings: stamp down the wretched and the weak: this is the law of the strong: this is our law and the joy of the world.

In III: 18, direful instructions are also given by Ra-Hoor-Khuit:

Mercy let be off: damn them who pity! Kill and torture; spare not; be upon them!

These instructions—which are very dangerous indeed as their literal interpretation would damn to hell anyone following it—nonetheless refer to the attitude that the soul must adopt in order to overcome the pull of her elemental nature, and so become a suitable vehicle for the Word of her True Will. There is in all times a war in heaven to be enacted upon earth for the soul who would be the winner of 'Ordeal x'. In other words, there is a Great Work to be done.

---

[127] The 'many and the known': Liber AL vel Legis, I: 10.
[128] III: 19.

Initiation of the Ka—The Alchemical Secret

Over thousands of years the ancient Egyptians developed complex doctrines concerning the various vehicles of spirit and soul, and their counterparts both in the macrocosm and microcosm. The symbolism by which metaphysical knowledge may be communicated is a vital part of the Great Work and a labour of love. The difficulty in using the Egyptian symbolism is that each *nome* centre—an earth location for a Neter (principle) or 'god' acting through nature—had its own cosmology, although there was no doubt a unified doctrine in the same way that there is in India, even today. In Liber AL vel Legis only the principles known as the Khabs, the Khu, and the Ka are mentioned directly. These are respectively the star (Khabs) as vehicle for the Holy Guardian Angel, the celestial body (Khu) and the subtle or vital body (Ka).[129] There is a fourth principle implied, as the nature of the Ka is dual: the Khaibet or 'shadow'—this term is used as the Egyptians literally depicted this principle as the shadow of a man.

I. The Egyptian word-symbol of the Ka is two upraised hands and arms. Its nature is double and is typified by the deities Horus and Set. In the non-initiate, the double Ka is housed—or imprisoned—by its feminine or passive counterpart, the Khaibet, which is depicted hieroglyphically as the shadow form of the person.

Any man or woman has a Ka and a Khaibet, but without yogic polarisation the Ka serves only the desire-impulses arising from the shadow, which absorbs environmental and inherited elements—these are, in the usual case, mistaken for the true Self by the ego (*ahankara*). The shadow is thus bound up with the human identity or ego. The Ka cannot then achieve its spiritual purpose by offering its substance to the Khabs so that it may be transmuted into a Khu body around that central 'star'.[130]

---

[129] The 'subtle body' is not really a body as such, as that only properly applies to the physical level. It is a convenience to call it 'body', as a figure of speech.

[130] The five-rayed Egyptian star is comparable to the *jivatma*, the centre of the 'creature self' or I-sense in yoga cosmology. It is only by meditating on the I-sense ('worshipping the star') that the higher knowledge (*boddhi*) is conveyed to the soul.

Only in this way is the star alchemically 'fixed', and therefore, by upward transposition, realised as identical to the true Self (Atma). Once initiation has truly taken place, the Khaibet, which has no integral reality or substance, drops away like a shell (*qlipha*) or husk. The dual principles personified as Horus and Set then divide or emerge from an undifferentiated state. Through self-polarisation, the flame of life called Hadit arises from the womb or tomb of matter and carries his seed of light-intelligence towards his Nuit or supreme state. The apparent ordeal of being 'torn upon wheels' has then to be passed through.[131] The breaking apart of the Khaibet is described as the swelling of Eucharistic bread or cakes of light.[132] The practitioner experiences this through the vibrations of the rising Serpent Power and the resulting phenomena—or emission of beetles, as it is described in the book. Such an emission also equates to the 'magical powers', and also the various *devas* and *asuras* (angels and demons), that come about spontaneously when yoga is practiced consistently and well.

II. The Ka in the normal state of affairs is a mass of appetites and desires that ultimately lead to dispersion and spiritual death. It seems that one can only either satisfy these desires—which is impossible, since their source is groundless—or attempt to keep them under control by suppressing them. It is clear that no attempt to suppress the appetites of the Ka by the way of moral rules of conduct has ever actually worked. Control can be enforced through severities, but the very severities then replace the appetites. Thus, throughout the Age of Iron or Kali Yuga, man has been his own jailer, torturer, and executioner.

III. There is a way out of this called initiation. Every truly initiatory path requires the highest standards of training and discipline. No trials are truly spiritual ones as they consist of opposition from within the person themselves, or otherwise environmental factors, but it all amounts to the same thing. However, unless the opposition within the self is mastered by the aspirant, no progress is made. In the majority of cases this threshold is never passed at all, for the appetites of the Ka are overwhelming and take on countless guises.

---

[131] Liber AL vel Legis III: 55.
[132] III: 25–29.

The successful aspirant, on the other hand, strengthens the Ka, making it fit for a Great Work through redirecting its hunger and thirst towards spiritual knowledge. In this way, the spiritual will is strengthened and the power of the shadow to absorb all the energy of the self is greatly weakened.[133]

IV. The Ka, at a further stage, is directed upwardly by the will. This can only take place once the dual Ka twins have been released from the Khaibet. In all traditions that have developed practical means for attainment, a symbol variously described as a body of light, chariot, or some other vehicle, is constructed by intelligent use of the will and imagination. The heart or centre of the body that has been identified with such a mandala may variously be termed as a pyramid, mountain, cave or labyrinth. The Ka then inhabits a Great Symbol of the Universe that is reflective of true principles. According to various traditions, such a Great Symbol is named Jerusalem, Abiegnus, Zion, Babylon, Adam-Kadmon, Sphinx, Phoenix, Ab-Hati, Duat, Aunnu (Heliopolis), or Nile. The notions of God, City and Man are combined in one symbol, which is built over a lengthy period of time and with detailed and painstaking care. Ultimately consciousness must extend in the six directions of space: North and South, East and West, Above and Below. The point of awareness is then placed in the exact centre (or heart lotus) of the three-dimensional cross thus formed.

V. The Ka can now be strengthened by various ways and means in its upward tending path. It is fed on nectar or ambrosia of the Gods, which is spiritual sustenance, as are the members of a spiritual Order once the Ka has been bound in service.

VI. The consciousness transferred to the Ka is seated in a chariot, so to speak, by which it is able to travel to places otherwise inaccessible to the human mind. To put this another way, individual possibilities are developed, through extension. The Ka now obeys the conscious will like a trained animal and takes pleasure in the exercise. It has lost its taste for the illusionary or 'weak' pleasures that captivate the earthbound soul. Gradually, delights of a metaphysical nature begin to become apparent.

---

[133] Cf. *Thunder Perfect Gnosis*, Part Two, which is concerned with the Raja Yoga of Patañjali.

VII. The Ka of an Initiate is double when it is fully polarised. The flame of Spirit-Fire has been awakened. This spirit-flame or seed of stars seeks its return through the veil of time and space to its source, its originality. The double at this stage can be realised, since it is fully polarised, as an earthly and a celestial Ka. The celestial aspect of the Ka is the Khu. The Ka and Khu are as the twin gods Set and Horus who preside over initiation, as indeed they always presided over the birth of a king. They are as the breath of spirit entering and leaving the nostrils of Ra, who in this case is a figure of Universal Man or the Integral Being.

VIII. The world of the Ka equates to that of Yetzirah in the Qabalah, while that of the Khu equates to the world of Briah, above the Abyss. The transformation of the Ka into a Khu establishes the birth of water mentioned in the Gospel of St. John (3: 1–21). The ordeals of initiation are described in Liber AL vel Legis, III: 63–67:

63. The fool readeth this Book of the Law, and its comment; and he understandeth it not.
64. Let him come through the first ordeal, and it will be to him as silver.
65. Through the second, gold.
66. Through the third, stones of precious water.
67. Through the fourth, ultimate sparks of the intimate fire.

The 'fool' of verse 63 is one that has not yet begun the path of initiation so is no different from any profane or common man.[134]

The ordeals of Set and Horus are described as silver and gold in verses 64 and 65. The elemental temptation of Set is to stay in a world of astral glamour and illusion; the spiritual temptation of Horus is to rule over the world using magical powers that correspond to Yetzirah, the astral plane or subtle realm. The angels of Yetzirah, whose heavily seductive realm must be passed through on the way to the celestial Khu, have their inverse reflection as devils or fallen angels, as are all those that minister to man and his Ka. He who fails to choose wisely falls into the 'pit called Because' (II: 27).

---

[134] Crowley wrote a comment, *Liber OZ*, a long time after Liber AL was first written. It was entirely the product of Crowley's socio-political fantasies, resembling a sort of 'Bill of Rights'; we cannot possibly take it seriously.

When the ordeals of silver and gold have been successfully passed, there follows birth or baptism of the celestial Khu, described in verse 66 as 'stones of precious water'. The astral body is discarded in so far as its glamour and seduction no longer enthral the Initiate. The consciousness is now able to fully enter the spiritual plane. The celestial water of Briah is that shown surrounding the god Amoun on Egyptian papyri, the Hidden God who comes forth in Silence. The accomplishment of the first three ordeals will automatically lead the practitioner to the knowledge described in verse 67, the 'ultimate sparks of the intimate fire'. While there can be countless flames or sparks, or countless souls, every flame is a particular modification of fire; every soul is a particular modification of Universal Being.

IX. A crossroads of the soul is arrived at with each ordeal. To master the astral or subtle plane, the practitioner learns to deal with and transcend intensely dualistic realisations of good and evil. In spite of the atmosphere of truth, holy awe and religious devotion that may very well accompany such realisations, none of them are in fact true; certainly they are not what is called the Real (Atma) or true Self.

Any dualistic phenomenon is a product of mind, and of the mind's encounter with that which is beyond it. Here is the primary 'ordeal' as typified by the temptation of Christ Jesus by Satan, who is an angel sent by God to test him, in the wilderness. The forty days spent in the desert corresponds Qabalistically to the Hebrew letter Mem (מ), which means, 'water'. The word-symbol for this letter is the Hanged Man of Tarot, showing forth in detail the nature of this initiation. An adept is one that has become the master of time and space. The figure of the Hanged Man has not been hanged as such, but he is suspended upside-down between the worlds; he is neither fully in the world of spirit, nor is he fully immersed in the waters 'below', which he knows by now to be a deception.[135]

The purpose of the Great Work as expressed in the language of alchemy is to give birth to, or otherwise to 'fix', an immortal stone. This is an individuality that is both one as self polarised and none as made of two distinctly different but un-manifested principles. Within the supreme principle there is difference but no separation:

---

[135] The meaning of this image goes beyond the mere cyclical or seasonal recurrence of vegetable life that is frequently put forward as an explanation for it. Likewise, perplexing chthonic items dug up from the past are invariably described as 'fertility gods' by those whose minds can reach no further than a naturalistic interpretation of all ancient symbolism.

> *The Perfect and the Perfect are one Perfect and not two; nay, they are none!*[136]

Once duality is abolished, so is the possibility of anything finite, as the finite only exists by virtue of its opposite. Therefore the reality that is veiled by the metaphor of the star or Khabs is unlimited—which is to say it is not subject to any determination.

X. Who accomplishes this is 'chosen' of Nuit. They may then manifest the True Will even while living in a body of flesh, upon the earth. There is nothing to be gained by looking for psychological or other remedies that require, and search for, a cause within the human individuality (*ahankara*) itself. The pursuit of objects to cleave to the self is the root of all that afflicts the human soul, since it results in the word of Sin that is the Restriction of the True Will:

> *The word of Sin is Restriction.*[137]

There is, however, a hidden assistant, a secret means. Such a means is secreted within the nature of love herself, which is the desire to unite with that outside or beyond the self. When the desire to unite, no matter what, is transferred to the love of wisdom and the wisdom seed, then the desire of the Ka, symbolised as the magick wand or caduceus of Hermes, the magician, is brought to the Great Work, the quest for the Holy Grail. Therein is the fulfilment of the Hermetic Arcanum, in which is perfect peace, everlasting joy and infinite bliss:

> *Love is the law, love under will.*[138]

---

[136] I: 45.
[137] I: 41.
[138] I: 57.

The Stele of Revealing (reverse)

Appendices

Restoration of the Sphinx

Like the Word, the Sphinx is periodically lost under the desert sands. Major works of restoration of the Egyptian Sphinx have been undertaken on six occasions in history. The timing of these closely coincide with major events in the history of the divine covenance. Thothmoses first restored the Sphinx around the year 1400 BC at the beginning of the New Kingdom. The Sphinx was at that time buried up to her neck in sand. Thothmoses had a dream in which the Sphinx asked him to free her from the sand, offering him as a reward the crown of Upper and Lower Egypt. This period of history coincides very closely with that of Moses reception of the law at Sinai that formed the basis of the old covenant (from the Christian point of view).

The second restoration works took place in about 500 BC when parts of the Sphinx were rebuilt. This coincides with the time of the end of the Kingdom of Judah and of the Egyptian Dynasties; it was around this time that Ankh-af-na-khonsu of the *Stele of Revealing* was a priest in Thebes.

The third restoration consisted of major excavation works that the Romans undertook at the beginning of the Christian era.

The Sphinx was once more excavated in 1926. The 1926 works of restoration had severely damaging effects on the monument, as did the subsequent (fifth) restoration that took place between 1955 and 1987. These twentieth century undertakings could be considered as a particular manifestation of the System of Antichrist near the end of time. The anti-word disrupts and destroys order and harmony so that the reasoning faculty, for example, becomes cut off from the heart intelligence and even ordinary conscience. In the wider sense, the errors that have quite literally broken the heart of the Sphinx have resulted from the complete loss of spiritual knowledge from modern science and industry.

The sixth and latest restoration work from 1989 seems to have alleviated the adverse effects of the twentieth century 'restorations'. This was initiated by an investigation aimed at a more complete understanding of the relationship between the monument and its environment. This latest project is said to have been completed in 2015, but we do not know how reliable such information is, or how this project is faring today, especially taking into consideration the political changes that have taken place since then.

Sphinx: Chronological Table

4000 BC ♉	Beginning of the precessional Age of Taurus and present Age of Kali Yuga.
3000 BC	Beginning of the Historical Period: as defined by the emergence of writing properly, so called, in about 3000 BC. Unification of Egypt as the Old Kingdom. Memphis is capital city. Canaanites; Abraham's ancestors as nomads in Mesopotamia.
2000 BC ♈	Beginning of the precessional Age of Aries. Moses is said to have received the Law at Mount Sinai. Egypt: Middle Kingdom, approximately 2030–1720. Era of the Patriarchs, as described in Genesis 12–50. About 1850 BC: arrival of Abraham at Canaan (Genesis 12). About 1700 BC: the Patriarchs (supposedly) in Egypt.
1500 BC	Egypt: New Kingdom, 1560–715. Thebes is capital city. Thothmoses excavates the Sphinx at Giza. Akhenaten (1377–1358) establishes exclusive worship of the Aten for a short time, the first anti-traditional attack. Tutankhamen (1358–1349). Amoun restored at Thebes. Seti I (1317–1301) Grandfather of Aiwass (Kha-em-uast). Rameses II (1301–1234) Father of Aiwass. 1250–1230: Jewish Exodus, as according to the Bible. 1230: Moses—the Law at Sinai, the Old Covenant.
1000–500 BC	1010–970: David. 970–931: Solomon marries pharaoh's daughter and builds the Temple of Jerusalem. 740: Call of the Prophet Isaiah. 721–587: End of the Kingdom of Judah. 800–500 BC writing of *Upanishads* in India, originally an oral tradition as with the *Vedas*, of which they are the completion. 663–525: XXVIth Egyptian Dynasty, the last before the Persian dominion; cult of Ankh-af-na-khonsu. 627: Call of the prophet Jeremiah. 622: Jewish Torah 'discovered' in the Temple of Jerusalem. 604–562: Nebuchadnezzar, king of Babylon.

	600: Ezekiel predicts the ruin of Jerusalem.
	587: Capture of Jerusalem: destruction of the Temple and city.
538–333 BC	500: Restoration of the Sphinx on Giza Plateau.
	Egyptian Restoration to Persian Period.
	525–400: Egyptian XXVIIth Dynasty—Persian domination.
	520–515: Building of the second Temple of Jerusalem.
	336–323: Alexander the Great.
333–63 BC	Hellenistic Period in Egypt.
	331: Foundation of Alexandria (destruction of old Aunnu).
1 AD ♓	39–4 BC: Reign of king Herod the Great.
	0–1 AD: The chronicled birth of Jesus of the New Testament.
	Roman Palestine.
	Beginning of precessional Age of Pisces.
63 BC–135 AD	The Romans excavate the Sphinx.
	Beginning of the Christian era; the symbol of Christ is the fish, indicating the relationship between that phase of history and the precessional Age of Pisces.
	Autumn of 27 AD: Preaching of John the Baptist and the beginning of the ministry of Jesus Christ.
	33 AD: The death of Jesus on the eve of the Passover.
1989 (modern era)	Latest restoration of the Sphinx.
	The modern era, towards the end of industrialisation and global expansionism—which includes mass propagation of Western anti-traditional and anti-intellectual propaganda.
2012–2020 ♒	The postmodern and post-industrial or technological era.
	Ending of the Great Cycle of the Ages according to the Mayan calendar ☉ ♑ Solstice 2012 AD.
	The restoration of the Sphinx is said to have been completed in 2015.
	The Fall of the Great Equinox; full commencement of the Reign of Antichrist and Apocalyptic era ☉ ♈ Equinox 2020 AD. Christ is largely denied in the West as are all religions and avatars. Ancient pre-religious traditions are by now interpreted by scholars on a basis of modern social and political fashions, including 'cognitive science', reducing all meaning to virtual zero.

Tree of Life: Principal Correspondences

Atu	Title	Letter	Value	Symb.	English	Path
0	Fool	Aleph	1	△	Ox (Plough)	11
I	Magician	Beth	2	☿	House	12
II	Priestess	Gimel	3	☽	Camel	13
III	Empress	Daleth	4	♀	Door	14
IV	Emperor	Tzaddi	90	♈	Fishhook	28
V	Hierophant	Vav	6	♉	Nail, pin	16
VI	Lovers	Zain	7	♊	Sword	17
VII	Chariot	Cheth	8	♋	Fence	18
VIII	Justice	Lamed	30	♎	Ox goad	22
IX	Hermit	Yod	10	♍	Hand	20
X	Fortune	Kaph	20	♃	Palm of hand	21
XI	Strength	Teth	9	♌	Snake	19
XII	Hanged Man	Mem	40	▽	Water	23
XIII	Death	Nun	50	♏	Fish	24
XIV	Temperance	Samekh	60	♐	Prop, crutch	25
XV	Devil	Ayin	70	♑	Eye	26
XVI	Tower	Pé	80	♂	Mouth	27
XVII	Star	Hé	5	≈	Window	15
XVIII	Moon	Qoph	100	♓	Back of head	29
XIX	Sun	Resh	200	☉	Head	30
XX	Judgement	Shin	300	△ ✹	Tooth	31
XXI	Universe	Tav	400	♄ ▽	Egyptian Tau	32

Hermetic Tree of Life

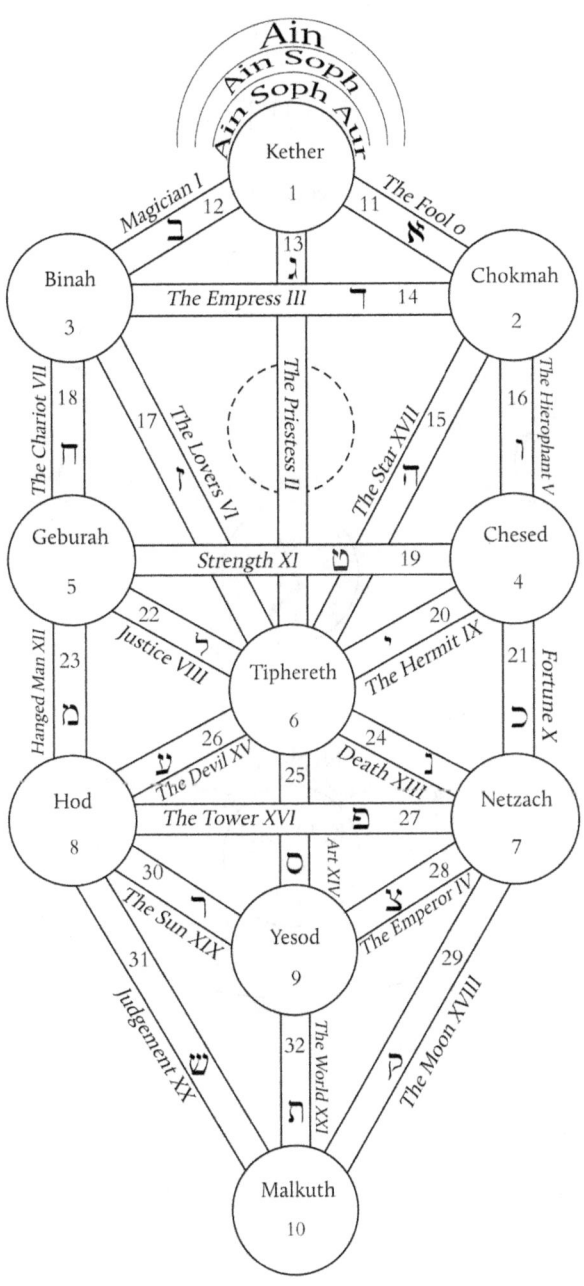

Tree of Microcosmos and Egyptian Parts of the Soul

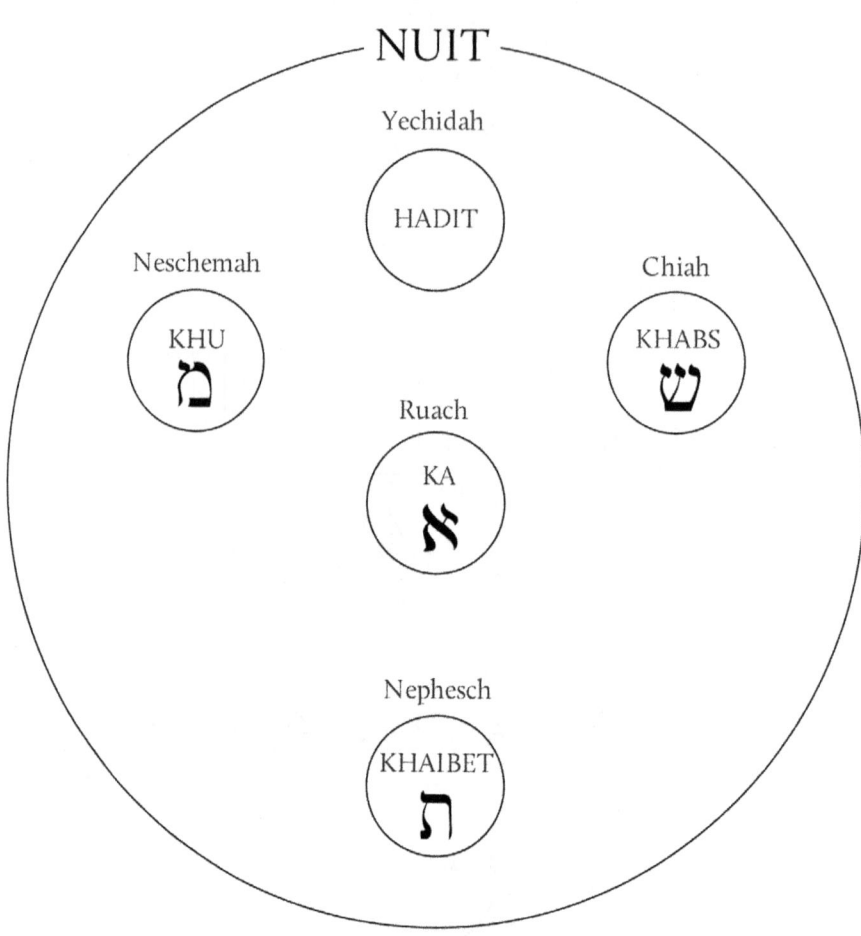

Tree of Life and the Four Worlds

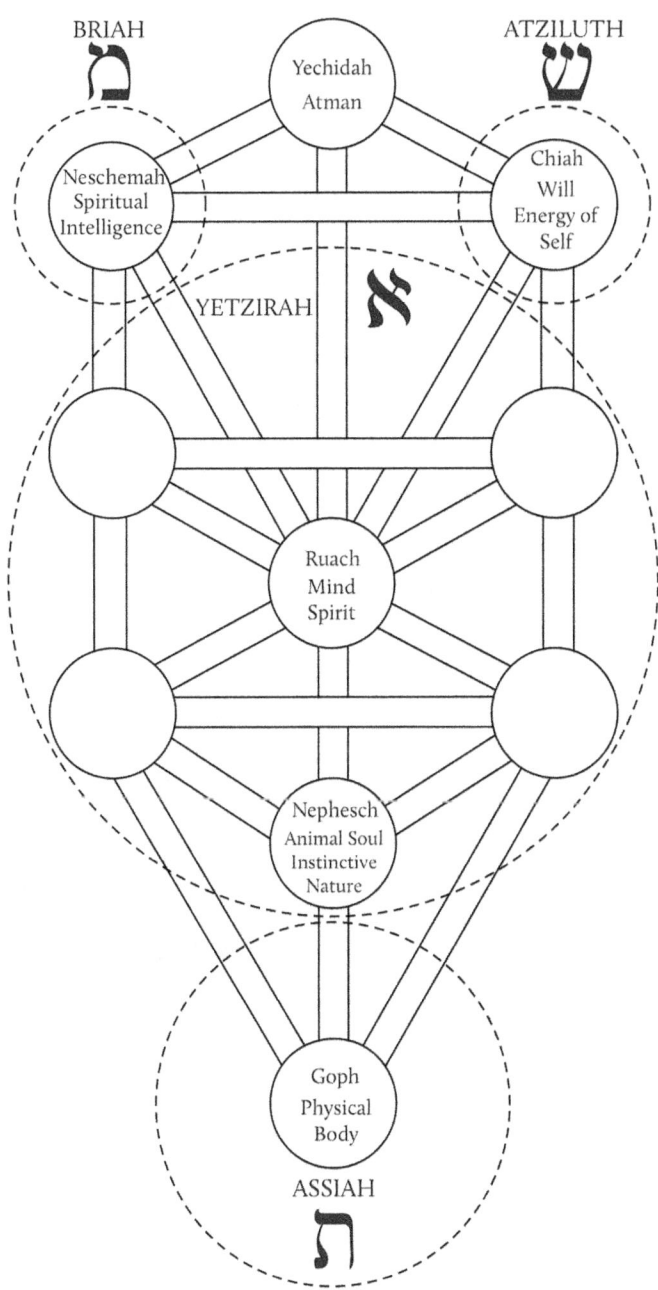

Glossary

Abrahadabra

The formula of the transfiguration of man's elemental nature into a Khu, the Holy Grail or celestial body in which Initiates are born forth to the stars of the body of Nuit. By Hebrew Qabalah the number of Abrahadabra is 418, the number of Nuit's love chant, 'To Me', which indicates to the Initiate where his destination lies. Abrahadabra is 'the reward of Ra Hoor Khut'. The reward is for those who are able to pass the ordeals of Ra Hoor Khuit, the Angel of the Last Judgement.

—See also Horus; Khu; Heaven, company of; Ra Hoor Khuit.

Abyss

The chasm through which consciousness 'falls' from union into duality. The nature of the Abyss is mind; its function is division. Out of it emerges the universe as perceived by the human mind that separates forms and defines them by contrast in order to know them—though this is an inferior knowledge as it rests on illusion. The division represented by the Abyss separates the Tree of Life from the Tree of Knowledge of Good and Evil, or Tree of Death. It separates macrocosm from microcosm, heaven from earth, and eternity from perpetuity. The Abyss is the lower (inferior) threshold of Qabalistic Da'ath, meaning 'Knowledge'. The superior Da'ath is hidden in the womb of Binah and is none other than the supernal Eden. The inferior Da'ath, which is the crown of a fallen universe, is the root of all 'death' which may be considered as physical or initiatory. In either case it constitutes a change in the state of the being. The relationship between knowledge and death as signifying a change of state in the being is made explicit by Hadit in II: 6, where he says: 'I am Life, and the giver of Life, yet therefore is the knowledge of me the knowledge of death.'

—See also Fall; Hadit.

Aeon (and Aeon of Horus)

The word aeon, meaning 'age' in Greek, refers to an indefinite period of time. It is sometimes taken as 'eternity' in philosophy, but this is incorrect as nothing in manifestation, even a Cosmic Cycle, can be eternal or infinite, which is something that can only be said about the supreme principial reality, permanent and not changed by anything from 'outside' Itself.

There is also a particular and technical meaning of 'Aeon' (or Aion) in that it can refer to a Master in certain Greek, Gnostic and Persian cults (Mithras being one of them). It is a heirophantic function but such a Master does not manifest an Aeon in terms of a Cosmic Cycle. According to Gnostic source texts, the universe manifests through Aeons, each of which consists of a male and female pair or *syzygy*.

The ('New') Aeon of Horus is an invention of Aleister Crowley and it does not correspond with any real measure of time or traditional theory of Cosmic Cycles. In a sense, Horus, as Ishvara, Lord of the Universe or Universal Man, is Lord of all Aeons, most particularly of the present Manvantara, which is now drawing to a close with the final and darkest Age of Kali Yuga.

—See *Nu Hermetica—Initiation and Metaphysical Reality*, 'Cosmic Cycles'.

—See also Horus; Heru-ra-ha; Thelema.

Ahathoor (Hathoor or Hathor)

Hathoor is the Egyptian goddess worshipped especially at Aunnu (Heliopolis), where she represents the (earlier) aspect of Isis who gave birth to Horus without the need for any paternal intervention. Ahathoor is also the mother of the star Sirius or Sothis. Her name literally means 'House of Horus' (Het-hor); as his dwelling she is his Khu, and Horus is her Khabs. This identifies Horus, as Khabs, with the star of Set or Sept, as the only begotten son of his mother, the Holy Virgin. The Egyptian star, with its five rays, is comparable to the Sanskrit *jivatma* with its five *tanmatras*, roots of the elements, upon which perception forms its basis. By upward transposition, this 'star' is realised as the reflection of Atma, the True Self, through the higher intellectual intuition—which is not in any way either sense or cognition and is properly speaking the intermediary between Heaven and Earth, to use symbolic terms. Hathoor is all of this.

The Greek name of Hathoor is Aphrodite, the goddess of love; her Roman name is Venus, and to the Greeks she was Astarte. Esoterically, the planet Venus is considered to emanate from the star Sirius—or from the point of view of earth, the celestial path of Venus crosses that of Sirius. Hathoor is the prototype of the Scarlet Woman or soul. As the soul in the underworld, she is usually depicted wearing scarlet; in her celestial aspect she is naked and clothed with stars, thus closely identified with Nuit.

—See also Aunnu; Chakra; Horus; Khabs; Khu.

Aiwass (or Aiwaz)

The praeterhuman intelligence that transmitted Liber AL vel Legis to Aleister Crowley in Cairo in 1904 through the mediumship of his wife (at the time), Rose—as according to Crowley.

By Hebrew Qabalah, the number of Aiwaz is 93, the number of Thelema, the 'word of the Law' given in Liber AL vel Legis, I: 39. By Greek Qabalah, Aiwass adds up to 418, the number of the 'reward' of Ra Hoor Khut, Abrahadabra.

Aiwass introduces himself as 'the minister of Hoor-paar-kraat' in I: 7, the only verse of the book where he is clearly speaking about himself. That is, he is the silent or emergent form of Horus, depicted as a child. Aiwass, as the son of Rameses II (Kha'm'uast), was entitled to wear the forelock of Hoor-paar-kraat (Harpocrates). Only a high priest of royal birth was entitled to wear the forelock. Only such could be a 'minister' or hold the priestly office.

However, the identity of Aiwass when he lived his life in mid to late dynastic Egypt was never known to Crowley and will never be known by those who believe Crowley, who claimed that Aiwass was 'his' Holy Guardian Angel, although he never received any further contact. Later, Crowley regarded Satan as his Holy Guardian Angel—which is equally preposterous although it is true that the Devil has his own angels to delude men, as according to scriptural law.

—See the chapter, 'The Holy Guardian Angel'.

—See also Abrahadabra; Heru-ra-ha; Holy Guardian Angel; Ra Hoor Khuit; Thelema.

Alchemy

The word 'alchemy' was derived from Khem, the 'black land' of Egypt. The degradation of alchemy through separation from any spiritual principle was the origin of the profane science of modern chemistry. The symbolism of alchemy has also been misconstrued as indicative of physical 'process', or even psychological process. It is best understood as metaphysical analogy, and by that we mean pure knowledge, not the 'abstraction' that has become the conventional meaning of the term. The following concerns the three primary alchemical principles, Sulphur, Mercury and Salt:

Sulphur is the radiating force; it always transmits its rays outward from the centre, from within. It has a correspondence with the will, so long as that is understood, for the purposes of the practice, in the sense of Divine Will or ordinance, which has nothing at all to do with the psychological or personal will-determination.

Mercury is as *yin* to the *yang* of Sulphur; it is nearly always regarded as a reflective feminine or aqueous principle—this is figured in the Tarot, where the Priestess II is the 'higher moon', alchemical Mercury and also the letter *gimel*. Salt is 'body' and is fixative or stabilising.

When we arrange these principles vertically, an interesting and useful symbol emerges. Sulphur as the 'spirit-fragrance' is placed centrally, and we must remember it acts on the other two—none of the principles are separate in nature. Mercury ☿ is then placed at the top and Salt ⊖ at the bottom. We can place with this the square or cube. The symbol of Sulphur 🜍 is sometimes represented by a square or cube surmounted by a triangle or pyramid. In the early stages of the work, the active Sulphur works on Salt to overcome inertia. But in the later stages, once the first Mercury has appeared, then Sulphur works on Mercury and creates the 'double Mercury', which is also likened to the universal solvent or agent, the Astral Light. The final stage is then to 'fix the volatile', which brings Salt into play once more. This produces the philosophic stone and simultaneously there is a return to the principial state, which is the goal of the Great Work.

Now it can be seen, as we have placed the principles here in a vertical column, that Mercury works inwards as a centripetal force, as opposed to Sulphur working outward from within. The combined action creates a movement. This can be posited by a wheel or circle around the three principles that is very much like the Wheel of Force, called 'Fortune' or sometimes 'Destiny' in the Tarot. Whichever way we see the direction of motion, there will always be an ascent of the circle on one side and a descent on the other. This is the ascending and descending force, which also equates to the two doors of the Lesser and the Greater Mysteries.

Ankh-af-na-khonsu

Ankh-af-na-khonsu was an ancient Egyptian initiatic cultic name adopted by certain priests and scribes of Thebes. The Ankh-af-na-khonsu priest of the *Stele of Revealing* lived in the XXVIth Dynasty. This relatively late Egyptian dynasty extended between the years 663 and 525 BC, a time in which the history of Egypt became increasingly merged with that of the Middle East and Greece.

Ankh-af-na-khonsu of the *Stele of Revealing* flourished at the same time as that of the Old Testament prophet Ezekiel, and the reign of the Babylonian King Nebuchadnezzar described at the beginning of the book of Daniel. This period of history coincides with the end of the Kingdom of Judah, which culminated with the Babylonian capture of Jerusalem and the destruction of the Temple in 587 BC. Ezekiel predicted these events around the year 600 BC, shortly after the alleged deportation to Babylon, a time at which the Temple had been taken over by 'pagan' cults. It is around this time also (in 622 BC) that the priest Hilkiah (see 2 Chronicles 34: 14 or 2 Kings 22: 8) claimed to have 'rediscovered' the Torah or Jewish Book of the Law in the Temple of Yahweh. Therefore a priest of Ankh-af-na-khonsu received the eschatological revelation recorded on his stele at a time that was very much heralding the end of an age. This marked the beginning of a tumultuous period that paved the way for the messianic era.

The name Ankh-af-na-khonsu refers to the moon god Khonsu.[139] Khonsu, whose name means 'traveller of the sky', was worshipped at Thebes as the son of Amoun and Mut. The name Ankh-af-na-khonsu literally means 'Life (*ankh*) of the traveller of the sky (*khonsu*)'. The Ankh-af-na-khonsu Initiate became the master of the forces of the underworld, overcame death and entered the immortal realm of the gods. Ankh-af-na-khonsu is referred to in the book as the priest of the princes, scribe and prophet. As a high priest in Thebes (Egyptian Waset), the 'place of ordinance', he was literally a priest to the princes, as he was expected to produce detailed knowledge concerning such things as royal births and the correct times for festivals and rites.

—See also: Nuit; Thelema; Set; Stele of Revealing.

Assiah (World of)

Assiah is the Hebrew and Qabalistic word for the fully manifested universe. Assiah corresponds to the sphere of Malkuth on the Tree of Life, the Kingdom. In Rabbinical Kabbalah it corresponds to the final letter Hé of Tetragrammaton (IHVH). The number of Assiah is 385, which is also the number of Shekinah, the divine feminine presence, or Holy Spirit, represented as 'light' or the Intelligible Light. The name Shekinah derives from *sakan*, meaning, 'to dwell, rest', and has an exact equation with the Shakti or divine power in Hinduism.

---

[139] By Hebrew Qabalah, Khonsu (ChNShV) adds to the number 364, a lunar number since it is that of the lunar year of 13 x 28 days.

In the context of Liber AL, the intelligence ruling over Assiah is the Scarlet Woman in the underworld or fallen universe.

See also the Scarlet Woman; Tetragrammaton; Worlds, Four.

Atziluth (World of)

Atziluth is the Hebrew and Qabalistic word for the supernal divine or archetypal world. It is frequently given as 'emanation', though this is more accurately 'essence', which owes to the etymology of the root Etz, 'essence', also the name for the Tree of Life itself, Etz Chaim. To the world of Atziluth are attributed all the names of divinity or God. It corresponds in Rabbinical Kabbalah to the sphere of Chokmah on the Tree of Life, and the tip of the letter Yod of Tetragrammaton (IHVH). It it thus an expression of the supreme principle and for that reason is sometimes ascribed to Kether.[140] The word Atziluth adds to 537, which is the number of the word for 'uterine aperture'. Atziluth is thus comparable with the ancient Egyptian hub of the universe, represented by the goddess Taweret in the form of a hippopotamus. On the ascent of the Tree of Life, passing through this aperture means leaving the worlds of manifestation altogether. In the context of Liber AL, the intelligence ruling over the world of Atziluth is the Beast, the life-giving spirit manifested as the centre of consciousness or star called Khabs.

—See also Beast; Khabs; Tetragrammaton; Worlds, Four.

Aunnu

At Aunnu (Heliopolis or On), Atum-Ra was the name given to the hidden power that stands behind Creation.[141] The name 'Atum' is very close to the Sanskrit Atma, which is not a 'creator' but the supreme individual principle, which must be realised as not separate from the impersonal Brahma. To exist as distinct from the undifferentiated waters of the Nun, Atum has to emerge through distinction—thus Atum 'becomes'. The Pyramid Texts describe this in the following terms:

---

[140] In this context Atziluth—and by further extension, the 'Beast' as Logos—represents the principle of the cosmological universe only.

[141] It should be noted that we use 'creation' as a conventional term, but in reality God does not make the world with his own hands. Manifestation comes about owing to the presence of the supreme principle but the idea of 'creation' owes purely to the anthropomorphisation of God that is unique to the Abrahamic religions.

> Hail Atum! Hail Khepri, He who becomes from Himself! You culminate in this your name of 'Mound', you become in this your name of Scarab-Khepri.[142]
>
> Atum-Khepri, you culminate as Mound, you raise yourself up as the Benu Bird from the *ben-ben* stone in the abode of the phoenix at Aunnu.[143]

Atum thus surges out of the Nun as the Primordial Mound. Atum is then said to respectively spit out and expectorate Shu (Air and Space) and Tefnut (Fire), the first two divine principles. Alternatively he brings the pair into the world by masturbating and causing 'the seed from the kidneys to come.'[144]

In another version of the myth, Atum is said to have created himself by the projection of his own heart, and to bring forth with him eight elementary principles with which he becomes the Great Ennead of Heliopolis: Shu and Tefnut, then Geb the earth, Nuit the sky, and finally Osiris and Isis, Set and Nephthys, the entities of cyclic life and renewal, of death and rebirth. 'None of them are separate from him', say the Pyramid Texts.[145]

Atum-Ra of Aunnu is the carrier of the invisible fire or seed, the metaphysical 'cause' of the first definition to arise from the Nun. He then brings forth from himself the nine divine principles (eight plus himself) that will order the Becoming.[146]

In the Pyramid Texts, this Great Ennead doubles, and then itself becomes a generative power: 'The King comes forth from between the thighs of the two divine Nines.'

See also: Hermopolis; Initiation—Egyptian centres of; Memphis; Thebes.

---

[142] Pyramid Text, 1587.

[143] Pyramid Text, 1652.

[144] This is, of course, a very literal Egyptological interpretation that rests on incomprehension. The 'kidneys' may simply be the testes, which would be the obvious source of the seed in question; but in either case, physicality is used as metaphysical analogy. What we are concerned with is the principle that is able to produce a cosmos through the duality of self-polarisation.

[145] Pyramid Text, 1655.

[146] Notably, the number nine is that of any circumference, while ten is the centre. The circumference may also be viewed as eight, in which the ninth is the centre of the circle. The number eight in all traditions indicates the cosmological sphere as it is a doubling of four, the foundation.

Ba

The Egyptian name for the soul of man, and for the World Soul. The Ba is usually depicted as a bird with a human face. The goddesses Isis and Nephthys frequently took on this form, representing the dual nature of the soul.

—See also: Scarlet Woman; Soul.

Babalon: See Scarlet Woman

Beast

The name 'Beast' is particular to St. John's book of Revelation, in which it is given to the power who, with the 'Scarlet Woman', rules over the material universe. Revelation refers to him as the beast 'who was, and is not' (Rev. 17: 10), indicating that he is the power passing in and out of manifestation through the Abyss. The word 'Beast' is also related to the name of a very ancient god called Bes, whose origin we cannot know for certain, and that is represented by a dwarf with a large head. Bes, 'the aged one who makes himself young again', can be dated to at least the earliest Egyptian dynasties. During the time of the New Kingdom of Egypt Bes became identified with Horus the child, Hoor-paar-kraat. Little by little Bes was merged with other forms of the solar gods until at length he absorbed the qualities of Horus, Ra and Tum. As such, Bes also moved into close relationship with Hrumachis, the Sphinx.

The Beast, Bes, the Sphinx, Horus and others are all expressions of the Intelligible Light—the transformative power hidden in Nature, animating her with a life that is cyclical. By the XXVIth dynasty, the time of the *Stele of Revealing*, Bes was wholly identified with Horus, with whom he shared the attribute of Lord of all Typhonian Beasts.

The Beast is thus the manifestation of Hadit, and has a dual nature. Above the Abyss, the Beast is the supernal Khabs, the utterer of the Word. The Hebrew word for 'beast' is *chi*, meaning 'alive, flowing'. Chi is the root of the Hebrew word *chiah*, which is the vital 'breath' or force somewhat akin to the Sanskrit *prana*.

Through the 'fall', the Beast becomes the spiritual counterpart of the natural soul. From him emanates the unseen breath, fragrance or intelligence that gives her life. He is the Khabs hidden in creation, his power coiled and contained within the soul to sustain her life. Liber AL vel Legis describes the Beast as 'ever a sun'. As a sun, the Beast is the Word, the supreme cosmic power and no different from Ishvara (Sanskrit), the Lord of the Universe.

He is the all-seeing divinity, the heart of the cosmos and the intelligence of the world. He is the blood of life, and as such, the appointer of life and death.

—See also: Khabs; Ruach; Scarlet Woman; Soul.

Bes: See Beast

Briah (World of)

The name given to that which is often termed the 'creative' world in the Qabalah, although the name has associations with 'abode', as with the Shekinah, and also 'honey', which is a type of essence that is always used to symbolise immortality. It is thus traditionally the abode of the Archangels. The world of Briah corresponds to the sphere of Binah on the Tree of Life, and through inference is the palace of light or temple that sustains all. In Rabbinical Kabbalah, Briah corresponds to the first letter Hé of Tetragrammaton (IHVH). The number of Briah is variously 217, or 218. The latter is also the number of the Hebrew words for 'moon' and 'multitude', two ideas closely associated with the Scarlet Woman, and of the Hebrew word for 'ether'. The ether is the 'upper air' of the Greeks, in other words, heaven. The word 'ether' is derived from the Greek *aithein*, meaning 'burn' or 'shine'. This relates Briah to the celestial or heavenly body called the Khu, meaning the 'shining one'. The Scarlet Woman in her celestial aspect thus corresponds to Briah.

See Heaven; Khu; Scarlet Woman; Worlds, Four.

Chakra

The chakra is a Sanskrit word meaning 'wheel' or 'circle'. It is used to describe subtle centres of force through which the *prana* is organised and distributed in the macrocosm and in the microcosm. Traditional Hindu yoga cosmology considers that there are six chakras in the human body; a seventh chakra is latent, and is placed outside the body, above the crown of the head. The *sahasrara* chakra flowers only when the dual forces within the soul obtain self-polarisation. The chakras are not really located 'in the body' and have no relation with physical organs or nerves, save by analogy, although in modern and especially New Age and neo-spiritualist writings the converse is often stated or implied. The chakras will be understood better if we think of them as representing states of consciousness.

See also Kalas; Kundalini.

Company of heaven: See Heaven

Chiah

In the Qabalah, the Chiah refers to one of the five parts of the human soul (see page 71). The word is derived from Chi, the Hebrew word for 'life, living, flowing', also any beast or creature. The Chiah is the part of the soul corresponding to Chokmah on the Tree of Life, the sphere of wisdom (Called divine Sophia by the Greeks). Chokmah is the sphere of the Beast in his superior aspect as the life-giving spirit and transmitter of the Word or True Will (in the microcosm). The Chiah and the sphere of Chokmah both correspond to the world of Atziluth. They are representations of the centre of consciousness called Khabs in Liber AL vel Legis, in its cosmic aspect.

—See also: Beast; Khabs; Soul.

Crater Cup

The Crater Cup is a term used in the Bacchic Mysteries to refer to the place of incarnation of the soul. The soul passes through various states of being and then to physical existence by descending into the Crater Cup, represented astrologically by the space enclosed between the zodiacal signs of Leo and Cancer. In the twelve-fold cycle of ascent and descent symbolised by the precession of the equinoxes, the Crater Cup corresponds to the 'first hour' (see page 30). In the Crater Cup, the dual aspects of the soul are undifferentiated. The purpose of the Great Work is to first separate these twin principles so that they may polarise each other, their relationship giving birth to a third principle transcending them both: an immortal star or Khabs, so the Crater Cup is transformed into a Khu.

—See also: Khabs; Khu.

Da'ath: See Abyss

Fall

In the Garden of Eden above the Abyss, the 'two' are in perfect union. The Serpent of Knowledge breaks forth as the Abyss, creating a world through division. The motion of the Serpent—which in the higher aspect is as the circle moving about the metaphysical 'point' in the centre—brings about the shift in consciousness through which the Scarlet Woman and the Beast, also depicted as Eve and the Serpent, are precipitated into the Abyss, wherein is the knowledge of good and evil—the duality that creates the relative illusion of world appearance and of their separation from each other.

The 'fall' manifests the Scarlet Woman as Assiah, the material and visible world, the base of the Tree inhabited by man, demons, and the Qliphoth or shells of the dead. Coiled within her dwells the power of Hadit given her by the Beast, the Kundalini or Serpent Power that has the potentialiaty of awakening her from the fall or descent into matter. The fall manifests the Beast as Yetzirah, the subtle formative world that is hidden within the Scarlet Woman.

Divided from spiritual consciousness by the fall, the Scarlet Woman loses the knowledge of the Word or True Will hidden within her. She can only become free from ignorance, sin and death by reuniting her consciousness to the word or Spirit concealed within her.

—See also: Assiah; Beast; Hadit; Kundalini; Qliphoth; Scarlet Woman; Yetzirah.

Hadit

Hadit is the complement of Nuit, whom he manifests as a celestial body of stars or radiant Khu. As such, he is the movement of a circle around a pole, 'point' or axis. He is the utterer of Nuit's will and her only son or 'child', called Yechidah in the Qabalah and Atma in Sanskrit. By contraction within the body of Nuit, Hadit begets subtle centres of consciousness called Khabs or stars. In these he dwells as the life-giving Word or True Will. The radiations emanating from the Khabs transmit intelligence and Will throughout the body of Nuit, the Khu that surrounds and sustains all. As movement, Hadit is the One Who Goes Forth, the verb, the Word.

Hadit is Life and the giver of Life, two principles that he manifests as the Scarlet Woman and the Beast. By Qabalistic Gematria Had is equal to 10 and therefore Iota or Yod, the secret seed, 'point' or *bindu*. He is thus the expression of Atma, in the perceptible world. He is the Knower, and knowledge itself, the serpent whose motion precipitates life across the Abyss, which is the universe subject to life and death.

The Egyptians portrayed Hadit as a winged globe or sun disc, usually with upraised uraeus serpents on either side. The wings show the mode of action or going forth. They convey movement upon the air or ether, thus introducing the idea of the life-giving breath of God or Gods—for example, the Elohim mentioned in the opening verses of the biblical book of Genesis.

The twin serpents are the symbol of duality, the root of all world appearance. They are also the principle of generative power, the undulatory movement that begets time and spatial consciousness. The disc itself is identified with Ra, the sun god; it is a stellar symbol showing the cosmic nature of Hadit.

In ancient Egyptian folk tales, Hadit portrays the heroic conqueror of the foes of Ra the sun god. Regarded esoterically, Hadit is the fire of life or Serpent Power. Hadit is the transformer of the energy of the self otherwise bound up or restricted in the elemental nature of man. He is able to accomplish this through the mode of burning up and transfiguring the substance of the soul.

The awakening of the Kundalini in the non-initiate can give rise to an exaggeration of the ego complexes or aggregates of elemental force that are bound up by the principle of attachment and limitation. This is spelled out in the warning given by Hadit in Liber AL, II: 26–27. It is seldom realised, in modern occultism at least, that the awakening of the Kundalini or Serpent Power, by whatever means, does not in an way constitite initiation. When carefully directed, it can act as a support to initiation, but it does not in itself confer it. By this error, many fools have fallen into a trap they are unable to escape from.

—See also: Heaven; Khabs; Khu; Kundalini; Nuit; Yechidah.

Hathoor: See Ahathoor

Heaven (and company of heaven)

Heaven is the celestial world, and world of the immortals, in contrast with the terrestrial world that is subject to time and death. Thus in all traditions there is Heaven and Earth, which require an intermediary to unify. Hadit manifests Nuit as a living body, the company of heaven or celestial Khu, also called the 'Scarlet Woman' in Liber AL vel Legis. The body of Nuit is the heavenly worlds that are referred to as Briah in the Qabalah. The word 'body' is here best understood as representing an intelligent formation of individualities or 'stars' gathered around a transcendent principle: manifesting the Word of Nuit, which is the True Will.

—See also: Khabs; Khu; Scarlet Woman.

Heliopolis: See Aunnu

Hermopolis

Hermopolis was the city of Hermes-Thoth, the master of magick, writing, numbers, measurement and time. It was the centre of instruction concerned with the description of the Nun, embodying its qualities and characteristics. Its metaphysics tells us that the primal Ogdoad or Eight was formed from the body of a sacred child who issues forth from a lotus in the middle of the Nun, the indefinable 'substance' that is the source of all manifestation or existence.

The Nun is envisaged as swampy mire; a seething primal cradle in which live four couples of serpents and frogs. Their names are Naun and Naunet, meaning both 'the initial waters' and 'inertia'; Heh and Hehet, meaning 'spatial indefinitude'; Kek and Keket, 'the darkness', and Amoun and Amounet, 'that which is hidden'. Niau and Niaut, 'the void' (a figurative term) or 'limitless expanse', sometimes replace Amoun and Amounet.

The primordial Eight or Ogdoad as envisaged at Hermopolis form a single entity:

> You [the Eight] have made from your seed a germ [*bnn*], and you have instilled the seed in the lotus, by pouring the seminal fluid; you have deposited it in the Nun, condensed in a single form, and your inheritor takes his radiant birth under the aspect of a child.[147]

The child coming forth from the primordial lotus is Ra, the principle of light itself, whose fathers and mothers are the Eight.

—See also: Initiation, Egyptian Centres of; Ra; Thoth.

Heru-ra-ha

Heru-ra-ha is the Egyptian double god whose twin aspects are Hoor-paar-kraat, or Pure Being (Universal Man), and Ra Hoor Khuit, the Lord of the manifested universe. These twin aspects are similar to those embodied by the twins Set and Horus. Set and Horus (Egyptian Heru) are sometimes represented, notably, at Aunnu, as the double god Heru-Set who, like Heru-ra-ha, stands as a bridge across the Abyss, invisible and visible, dwelling in both formless reality and in the formal world subject to time and space. Heru-ra-ha—sometimes simply called Horus, although there are many Horus gods—is the god presiding over the aeonic pair or *syzygy* in which dwell the souls of the 'Imperishable Ones', abiding forever in the body of Nuit.

---

[147] Edfu VI: 11–12, and Esna V: 263.

Heru-ra-ha is the guardian of the great threshold called the Abyss, and Lord of the Last Judgement. Qabalistically, the name Heru-ra-ha adds to 418—see 'Abrahadabra'.

—See also: Aeon; Hoor-paar-kraat; Horus; Nuit; Ra Hoor Khuit; Set.

Holy Guardian Angel

The Holy Guardian Angel can be understood in one sense at least as the spiritual counterpart of man's natural soul, as seen from the corporeal point of view. Seen from this point of view, which is also that of the natural soul or of dualistic human consciousness, the Angel is an objective being. Like the Egyptian god Set, he is always where consciousness is *not*. The manifestation of the Angel is what the ancient Egyptians called a Khu; his heart (intelligence) they called a Khabs.

In the Four Worlds of the Qabalah, the natural soul, known to the Egyptians as the Ka, is fallen and dwells in Assiah, the material world. The Angel then rules over Yetzirah, the subtle formative world. In Thelemic terms, the Angel's function is to receive the Word of the True Will and communicate it to the natural soul. For such communication to take place, the soul has to unite with the Angel in love under will—the instruction given by Nuit in Liber AL vel Legis. Through this union, the Holy Guardian Angel consumes the life and substance of the natural soul or Ka.

Thus the substance of the natural soul is transmuted into a 'body' or housing for the Holy Guardian Angel, who would otherwise, like the Shekinah or Shakti, have no abode. This body or Khu is of the same essence as the body of Nuit, the company of heaven dwelling in the essential (or archetypal) world, Briah. The Angel and the soul then form one body and one spirit, a Khu and a Khabs. Their substance has become identical to that of the celestial Khabs and Khu, the worlds of Briah and Atziluth, into whose lives they are able to pass to be born forever as a star in the company of heaven.

The Holy Guardian Angel is a metaphor used by Iamblichus in his *De Mysteriis* for the being who is also referred to as the Augoeides, a Greek word derived from Augos, meaning 'morning light'. Other meanings are: Holy Ghost (or Spirit), Redeemer, Messiah, the Alpha and Omega (personified as a Word made flesh) or simply, the Way. In Liber AL vel Legis the Khu and the Khabs are also referred to as the Scarlet Woman and the Beast.

—See also: Beast, Fall, Ka, Khabs, Khu, Heaven, Scarlet Woman; Set.

Hoor-paar-kraat

Hoor-paar-kraat, which has various spellings and is also Harpocrates as known to the Greeks, is the Egyptian god of silence, the hidden aspect of the double god Heru-ra-ha and equivalent of the god Set. As latent and withdrawn or unextended, Hoor-paar-kraat is the dwarf-self, Holy Guardian Angel or Khabs who, when fertilised by the divine Word, comes to manifestation as his twin Ra Hoor Khuit.

—See also: Heru-ra-ha; Ra Hoor Khuit; Set.

Horus

Horus is the Greek form of the Egyptian god named Heru or Hoor (Coptic), of which there are many forms. Horus generally represents consciousness moving across time and space, transcending death. As such he is not only a 'saviour god' but is also concerned with the deliverance, known as *moksha* in Sanskrit, which is ultimate freedom from the perpetual wheel of birth and death.

Horus is 'that which rises up', which implies an ascent, descent and re-ascent, as is the case with an avatar, of which he is a type. The Egyptian name HRU (Heru) means 'countenance, face, sky, day'. It is composed of the letter H, the letter of breath and spirit, added to RU, 'mouth', therefore meaning 'breath of Ra'—which was indeed one of his many titles and attributes. The name Horus is related to the Greek word *hora*, meaning 'season, hour', which shows an aspect of Horus as marker of time—a more exoteric function.

Horus is the twin of Set. He is the solar consciousness emerging triumphant from the dark womb of his mother Nuit, Typhon or Draco. The victory comes after a long battle against the natural forces of dispersion embodied by the god Set, the opposer who perpetually attempts to slay Horus. Horus rules over both heaven and earth. His power is double, and its symbol is the Egyptian Sphinx. The Horus form most closely associated with the Sphinx is Hrumachis, one of the aspects of the god mentioned in Liber AL vel Legis. Other aspects of Horus are referred to as: Heru-ra-ha, Hoor-paar-kraat and Ra Hoor Khuit. Gods such as Tum, Ahathoor and Khephra are representations of various stages of the Horus cycle, as seen from the terrestrial or human perspective.

The ancient Egyptians attributed Horus to the planet Saturn. On the Tree of Life, Saturn corresponds to the sphere of Binah and the World of Briah, heaven. He is thus also the type of the Khu.

—See also: Aeon; Briah; Ahathoor; Heaven, Company of; Heru-ra-ha; Hoor-paar-kraat; Khephra; Khu; Nuit; Ra-hoor-khuit; Set; Sphinx; Thelema; Tum.

Hrumachis (Harmachis; Hormaku)

Hrumachis is the Greek name of the Egyptian god Heru-khuti, also known as Horakhyti, 'Horus of the two horizons', who represents the sun in his daily course across the sky from sunrise to sunset. Hrumachis is the god of the Sphinx, symbol of the duality of the manifested universe.

As the god of the two horizons, and with a human face and body of a lion, Hrumachis is the embodiment of the dual principles of love and power, wisdom and knowledge. He is also as Christ and the Virgin in one unified form. Various Horus gods such as Ahathoor and Ra Hoor Khuit are all forms of Hrumachis. Other Egyptian gods mentioned in Liber AL vel Legis such as Hoor-paar-kraat, Tum and Khephra, correspond to the invisible or un-manifested phases of the universal cycles, or the frontiers thereof. The Horus god who stands as a bridge between the worlds is Heru-ra-ha, a double god whose twin aspects are Hoor-paar-kraat (the invisible universe) and Ra-hoor-khuit (the visible universe). The chief shrines of Hrumachis were at Aunnu (Heliopolis).

—See also: Ahathoor; Heru-ra-ha; Hoor-paar-kraat; Horus, Khephra; Ra-hoor-khuit; Sphinx.

Initiation—Egyptian Centres of

Over the course of nearly three thousand years of history a myriad of initiation centres flourished in dynastic Egypt. Most were established along the Nile, which the Egyptians saw as a personification of the life current that sustains the universe. Five of these centres grew to be of particular importance in Egypt's history. Starting from Upper Egypt, these are: Thebes, Abydos, Hermopolis, Memphis, and Aunnu. Of these five centres, Abydos was the most exoteric. It was the seat of large public performances of the mysteries, and a popular pilgrimage centre. It was at Abydos that many of the complex and esoteric themes of other centres were presented to the populace. The primary deities worshipped at Abydos were Osiris and Anubis, as well as the god Khentamentiu who became gradually absorbed by the cult of Osiris.

Of perhaps greater esoteric significance were the mysteries of Thebes, Hermopolis, Memphis and Heliopolis (or Aunnu). Uppermost and furthermost is Thebes (Karnak), the centre dedicated to the gods Amoun, Mut, and their child Khonsu, the Moon. The work of the priesthood of Thebes involved the time cycles animating the living manifestation of the goddess symbolised there as the hippopotamus, mother, Apet. The Cosmic Cycles were understood to manifest the life of Amoun, the Hidden God, dwelling inside the goddess. Thebes was the centre that was most particularly concerned with the maintainance of communication between the eternal principle and earth, which is bound by time.

Next down the course of the Nile is Hermopolis, the city of Hermes-Thoth. Thoth is the god ruling over the principle of creation by division and doubling, through which the spirit acquires a shadow: matter, which is also the world of appearance (and therefore death).

The formation and transformation of 'substance' was the focus of the work performed at the next centre following the course of the Nile, Memphis. Memphis is situated at the crossroads between Upper and Lower Egypt. The subtle Ka was understood by the initiates of Memphis to be fashioned by the god Ptah-Sokar, the blacksmith who gives form and substance, and that conversely transfigures name and form back to the spirit.

Following Memphis comes Aunnu, the 'pillared city' where 'the King comes forth from between the thighs of the two divine Nines'. Aunnu (named Heliopolis by the Greeks) was located at the entrance of the Nile delta, across the river from the plateau of Giza where stands the Sphinx and the Pyramids. Aunnu was the physical location of the Primordial Mound, the place of birth of the Ever-becoming One and the point at which light enters the world. There, the Word was made flesh.

—See also: Aunnu, Hermopolis, Ka, Memphis, and Thebes.

Ka

The Ka is man's subtle force, which is the substance of the natural soul. The Egyptian hieroglyph of the Ka is two upraised hands and arms. In Egyptian symbolism the gods Set and Horus represent the dual Ka of the Initiate or King, and stand on either side of him. In the non-initiate, the double Ka is housed or imprisoned by its feminine counterpart, Khaibet, which is often depicted as a shadow form of the person.

Any man or woman has a Ka and a Khaibet, but without being polarised and thus liberated through initiation, the Ka is subject to desire-impulses arising from the shadow. The Khaibet, or shadow, is itself bound up with the human identity or ego—which is that part of the shadow that in the ordinary case we think of as being 'ourselves'. The Ka double cannot therefore achieve its spiritual purpose, which is to offer its substance to the Holy Guardian Angel or Khabs for the formation of a Khu, by which the Khabs star can be 'fixed'. Through repeated union with the Angel, the Khaibet, which has no essential reality or substance, drops away like a shell (*qlipha*) or husk. The liberated dual principles Horus and Set then divide. Through their polarity, they cause Hadit, the flame of life arising from darkness, to awaken and arise towards his Nuit or infinite bliss.

—See also: Holy Guardian Angel; Horus; Khabs; Khu; Qliphoth; Set.

Kalas

Kala means 'time' and is also a Sanskrit term indicative of the powers or emanations of the Shakti. Literally, a *kala* is an interval of 96 seconds. There are 15 *kalas* to a *ghari* of twenty-four minutes duration. The *ghari* is itself the equivalent in time of a course of *tattva-bhutas* that are five elemental modifications of *prana*. The *prana* is what the Egyptians called the 'breath of Ra', a subtle solar radiation that gives life and movement to things. In the Qabalah, this breath or life-giving spirit is called the Ruach. As the powers of the Shakti, and which may manifest in various forms such as *devas*, *devis* and *asuras* (male and female angels or devils), they are the radiations of Nuit, or from the Khabs or star dwelling in her celestial body, the Khu.

—See also: Khabs; Khu; Ruach.

Khabs

The Khabs is a centre of intelligence or light, transmitted throughout the Khu, the body or matrix that surrounds it. The Khabs is the 'house' of Hadit. It refers to the spirit called the Holy Guardian Angel in the Western Tradition. The Khabs corresponds, in its cosmic sense, to the Qabalistic world of Atziluth and the sphere of Chokmah. Through the fall, the Khabs becomes the heart (or Tiphereth) of the formative world of Yetzirah, and therefore of the Ruach also. It is the source of the spirit, intelligence or the subtle 'fragrance' animating creation. Khabs is an Egyptian word for 'star', though not a star as seen in the heavens at night, which is called *seba*.

More precisely, the Khabs depicts a portal or doorway in space through which shines the light of spirit. There is a subtle inference conveyed by the hieroglyphs: Khabs is the exact reverse or mirroring of the word Sbak. The latter depicts an aperture, opening or mouth that devours or consumes; as such it is a symbol of time but also eternity, for the hub of the (visible) heavens revolves about the Pole or supreme principle.

The devouring gods were also constellations. Sbak includes the word *seba*, which as previously explained has the meaning of a star in the literal sense. The star of the Khabs or Holy Guardian Angel is thus an inner doorway or aperture, a non-material means of ingress and egress between human and supra-human worlds. Abs, the reverse of Sba, star, is an 'abyss', which is really a figure of speech for the heart lotus as it is called in Hinduism, and which is the Seat of Brahma. This 'space' (an analogous term) is not truly empty at all, but is filled with *akasha* or ether, which has a close identification with spirit, as well as with speech and hearing or sonic and light vibration. This is confirmed by the fact that the word Ab signifies the heart, which the Egyptians understood as the seat of spiritual intelligence. The heart or Ab is that which reveals the soul, the Ba, through the inward direction of consciousness. Concentration is thus required for entering the true meditation state (*dhyana*), which itself is a preparation for Samadhi or divine union, the primary goal of yoga.

—See also: Holy Guardian Angel; Kalas; Khu; Ruach; Soul.

Khephra

Khephra is Ra, the sun god, in the form of the winged scarab beetle. The Egyptian metaphysical analogy tells us that in this way, Ra emerged from the primeval or undifferentiated 'substance' called the Nun—which is the near or even exact equivalent of Sanskrit *prakriti*.

Khephra is called the 'father of the gods' and the 'self-produced'. He not only produces himself, but also brings forth two deities, one male (Shu) and one female (Tefnut). As such, Khephra is the prototype of the androgynous god that is the principle of manifestation through parthenogenesis, which is also a form of self-polarisation. From the state of living 'seed' or latency in the abyss of Nu or Nun, Khephra emerges in the visible form of the rising sun. Khephra is thus also the symbol of resurrection, in which a living germ or seed of light passes to the immortal realm. The form of Ra with which Khephra is most closely allied is that of Hrumachis, the god of the Sphinx.

—See also Ra; Hrumachis; Nuit; Nun; Sphinx.

Khu

The Khu is an ancient Egyptian term symbolised by a large heron, phoenix or other fabulous bird with a long, curved beak. The Khu is a matrix formed around a centre of consciousness or light-intelligence called Khabs. The Word emanating from the Khabs is manifested and sustained by the Khu that contains it. In Liber AL, the celestial Khu refers to the 'company of heaven' or the heavenly body of Nuit as manifested by Hadit. As Life, the Khu is called the Scarlet Woman. In her dark or underworld aspect, she is manifested as the material world, Assiah, and the natural soul, called Nephesch in the Qabalah.

—See also: Khabs; Khu; Soul.

Kundalini

Kundalini is the Sanskrit word for the Serpent Power, depicted as coiled to show its latency. The life-giving power of Hadit is thereby transmitted to the Khabs or Holy Guardian Angel. In yoga, and most particularly the development of it called Laya Yoga, the vital force or Kundalini, that which keeps us alive, is said to be coiled at the base of the spine in the occult anatomy. The dream of existence and world appearance arises therein. The Shakti or living power, personified as a goddess (*devi*) of the same name, is able to rise upward along the path of the *shushumna*, or central canal, which has an equation with the 'middle pillar' of the Tree of Life in the Qabalah. The upward movement is facilitated by the *pranayama* or inward and outward breath in the yoga practice, combined with upward aspiration and sometimes use of various images (*yantras*) and sounds (*mantras*).

—See also: Hadit; Holy Guardian Angel; Khabs.

Maat (or Ma'at)

Ma'at is the Egyptian goddess of truth, justice, measure and balance. Her symbols are the flowering reed (sometimes feather or plume), and the scales. Ma'at presides over the universal equilibrium, and her law governs the Hall of Judgement in which the hearts or souls of the deceased are weighed and assessed. The souls found justified at the Judgement are those whose lives have been true to the divine Word or Will. The Egyptian Book of the Dead (so-called) calls these souls *maa kheru*, meaning 'he whose word is truth', which is a virtue attributed in Liber AL vel Legis to prophets such as Ankh-af-na-khonsu (Liber AL, III: 37). The utterer of the Word is the god Thoth or Tahuti, the male counterpart of Ma'at.

The Book of the Dead—more correctly, the Book of Coming Forth into Light—states that Thoth and Ma'at stand one on each side of the boat of Ra, the sun god in his aspect as universal consciousness, and take an important part in directing the course of the boat.

The letter 'L' (Lamed) was the original title of the (Egyptian) Book of the Law, and symbolises Ma'atian justice and thus peace. Lamed, the letter of the Law, is assigned to the twenty-second path of Libra on the Tree of Life. Venus rules Libra, whose letter is Daleth and whose Tarot image is the Empress IV. The path stretches between the twin terminals of Chokmah and Binah above the Abyss. Daleth or Venus thus unites and equilibrates primal polarity, while Saturn, which is exalted in Libra, dispenses justice. Ma'at embodies the principles of justice, truth and balance, overseeing the Judgement or equilibration of the soul that takes place through the Scales of the Balance of Libra. The close affinity between Ma'at as Justice and her consort Thoth as the Word is worth noting.

—See also: Ankh-af-na-khonsu.

Magick

The true principle of magick is the wisdom and science of the Magi—the wise men and women of old. The term is thus indicative in its highest sense of the ancient or perennial wisdom, handed down through the ages orally, and later written or inscribed in scriptures, talismans, hieroglyphs, runes, stones and stars. More generally, magick consists of traditional sciences, which are an application of metaphysical doctrines, though the very widespread use of what now passes for magick today either ignores or knows nothing of such doctrine and rests entirely on the use of syncretic correspondences.

Memphis

At Memphis, the universe is taken one stage further in the direction of name and form. Ptah, the divine blacksmith, himself becomes the primordial fire and gives it substance. The archetypes that were enunciated by Atum at Heliopolis are here materialised by Ptah. The Shabaka Text (710 BC) enumerates Ptah's eight hypostases or subtle qualities as 'the Neteru who have come into existence in Ptah'. He thus incarnates the primordial Eight, and then becomes Tatennen, 'the earth which rises up'—an evocation of the Primordial Mound. The same text continues: 'He who manifested himself has heart, he who manifested himself has tongue; in the likeness of Atum is Ptah, the very ancient one who gave life to all the Neteru.'

The heart and tongue of Ptah have power over all the other members, since the tongue describes what the heart conceives. Thus Ptah recreates the Great Ennead, the nine divine principles that are brought forth from the secret seed or fire of Atum—nine including himself. From the Ennead come forth all the qualities of things through the desire of his heart and the word of his tongue. The heart and tongue of Atum and Ptah are central to the Egyptian symbolism. They are referred to three times by Nuit in the first chapter of Liber AL vel Legis. It is said that the Ennead, which was the 'seed and hand of Atum', becomes the 'teeth and lips of Ptah' and gives a name to each thing, bringing it into existence.[148]

Divine principles and qualities can now 'enter into all species of things'—mineral, plant or animal—and become manifest through them. This is clearly an account of divine ordinance by the Word or Logos. Ptah, together with Sekhmet and Nefertum, constitutes the first causal triad. At Memphis, Ptah and Sekhmet were said to have given birth to their son Nefertum, the primordial lotus emerging from the void. Like the Sun, Nefertum opens in the morning and closes at night. The name Ptah means 'Foundation', viz., upholder and preserver of the primordial tradition. There is an associaiton with 'stone' or 'rock'—which was the attribute of Peter (or *pater*), the foundation of the Church as according to the New Testament. His was the Great Name of the Neter of Mennefer (Memphis), the capital of the dual Khemetic state for most of its history.[149]

Ptah is depicted as a mummified man wearing a skullcap and bearing the symbols of life, sacerdotal power and stability (*ankh, was, djed*) in his unfettered arms, standing on the plinth that forms part of Ma'at's hieroglyphic name. The plinth is identical in its meaning to the symbolic straightedge of freemasonry.[150]

---

[148] The Ennead is comparable to the nine spheres of the Tree of Life below Kether.

[149] Men-nefer means 'Justified Min', where the god Min refers to Osiris in his ithyphallic form.

[150] The skullcap worn by Ptah associates him with the skull or head, which is the centre of the primordial tradition or head of the polar axis. Like the cave, it is also a representation of the incarnated Word or Word made flesh, a doctrine associated with Christ. See John I: 14: 'And the Word was made flesh, and dwelt among us.'

Ptah is sometimes seen as a form of Atum, the Self-Created One, who effected creation through the actions of his heart, identified with Heru-Ur.[151] His tongue was identified with Tahuti, who 'set all the Neteru in their places and gave all things the breath of life'. As a creator, Ptah is far more directly involved with manifestation and ordinance than either Atum-Ra of Heliopolis, or Amoun, whose cult centre was at Thebes.

An earlier form of Ptah was Sokar. Ptah, Sokar and Osiris were later identified with each other, or were seen to represent different aspects of one principle, that of death and resurrection. The name Sokar (or Seker), means 'Pure One', by which it can be inferred that he is the principle of Pure Being, by which manifestation comes about but that is not involved in it in any way.

An obscure name in its beginnings, Sokar is depicted as a hawk-headed mummified man. He was originally Lord of both darkness and death, in the higher sense of the unmanifest, which nonetheless contains all possibilities of manifestation. This was particularly so in the region of Memphis and especially in Ankh-tawy, 'Lady of Life', a name given to the Memphite necropolis now known as Saqqara.[152]

Sokar eventually came to be viewed as a mysterious, chthonic form of Ptah, and in very late periods was thrice syncretised to become Ptah-Sokar-Osiris, the penultimate lord of death, judgement and burial. The sacred boat on which Sokar's icons were carried in procession (called *hennu*), is one of the earliest-mentioned of such boats in the Khemetic scriptures, and may have served as a model for later sacred barques. Sokar can be said to be the Hennu Boat itself.

—See also: Aunnu (Heliopolis); Hermopolis; Initiation, Egyptian centres of; Thebes.

Mentu

One of the names of the god Ra Hoor Khuit or Herukhuty. At Thebes, he was known as Mentu-Ra, a unified form of Ra and Set.

—See also Thebes; Ra Hoor Khuit.

---

[151] Heru-Ur is Horus the son of Nuit, the double god who looks both North and South.

[152] It is worth noting that the name 'necropolis' was bestowed by the Greeks at a relatively modern time, but the Egyptian name was about life, not death. Likewise, the false title of the Egyptian Book of the Dead was first given it by tomb robbers and later adopted by all Egyptologists.

Nephesch

In the Qabalah, the Nephesch represents one of the five parts of the human soul. On the Tree of Life it is attributed to the lunar sphere of Yesod and, in certain schemes, to the sphere of Malkuth. Nephesch is the Hebrew word for 'to take breath', and generally for 'soul' too, or any living creature. It is thus comparable to the Sanskrit *jiva*. The 'breath' taken in by the soul is the Ruach, the wind, scent, fragrance or spirit hidden in creation and giving it life. In the Hindu tradition, the breath animating the soul is called *prana*, which is manifested in time by the *kalas* of the Shakti power of the Lord of the Universe.

—See also: Kalas; Ruach; Scarlet Woman; Soul.

Neschemah

In the Qabalah, the Neschemah represents one of the five parts of the human soul. On the Tree of Life, the Neschemah is attributed to the sephira Binah, 'Understanding' or sometimes 'Mind', which does not represent the human mentality but the Intelligible Light. As the divine intelligence or higher intuition, the Neschemah is comparable with the Sanskrit *boddhi*. The Neschemah is thus the consciousness attributed to the soul or Scarlet Woman in her celestial aspect. By contrast, the Nephesch represents the consciousness of the Scarlet Woman in the underworld or fallen state.

Nuit

Nuit has sky and space as her visible symbols, which conceal the aspect of Nuit that is Absolute, and comparable to the Hindu Brahma 'supreme', or Brahma without attributes. Hadit, her complement on the cosmological level, manifests Nuit as a celestial body or Khu. Hidden within her, he is the utterer of her Word, which is in turn transmitted through subtle centres of consciousness called Khabs or stars. The radiations emanating from the Khabs transmit Nuit's sacred Word, summed up as 'love under will', throughout the Khu that surrounds and sustains them. Liber AL vel Legis also refers to the body of Nuit as the 'company of heaven'. Manifested as Life by Hadit, Nuit is called the 'Scarlet Woman', or otherwise Babalon.

By Qabalistic Gematria, Nuit adds to 75, equal to 'stars and space', and also 'the night'. The night, or dreaming consciousness aspect of Nuit, corresponds to that which lies outside the 'day' of the waking consciousness.

—See also: Hadit; Heaven; Khabs; Khu.

Nun

The Egyptian word for the primordial undifferentiated 'substance', of which the supreme unmanifest aspect is called Ain Soph in the Qabalah, 'Limitless Light'. Such a light is not visible or perceptible— we are in a relam where all terms are analogous. The lower aspect of this is 'chaos', a term used to denote undifferentiated 'matter', in a primordial state. There is thus a higher and a lower primordial state to take into account—this duality is frequently confused.

Pi (π)

Pi is the sixteenth letter of the Greek alphabet, used in mathematics as symbol of the ratio between a circle's circumference and its diameter. *Pi* therefore represents an essential component of the formula of the 'squaring of the circle'. This is expressed by the equation $\pi \times D = C$, or conversely, $\pi = C/D$.

Metaphysically speaking, the squaring of the circle represents the apparent division of the circle of 'infinity' by polar extension, by which the sum total of complementary dual principles comes about. *Pi* is a constant, indefinite number. It may be approximately expressed by the ratio of $22/7$, and is given to the sixth decimal place as 3.141593 by the riddle contained in Liber AL, III: 47. The solution of this riddle lies in the configuration of letters and numbers arranged in the grid that appears on page 16 of the book's manuscript.

—See *The Flaming Sword Sepher Sephiroth* (Second Edition Revised) for the complete solutions to all the riddles of the (Egyptian) Book of the Law.

—See also: Beast; Khabs; Khu; Kundalini; Ma'at; Scarlet Woman.

Prana

Prana is the Sanskrit word for 'breath', though it is much more than that and may be interpreted in the broadest possible terms, including breath of life, fragrance, or spirit animating creation. As such, *prana* is also 'food' or sustenance, and so it is said that '*prana* eats *prana*', so far as the corporeal plane is concerned. The movement of the *prana* is periodic as viewed from time and space, which is the particular human perspective; the elements of this periodicity are called *kalas*. The breath of life is called Ruach in the Qabalah.

—See also: Kalas; Ruach.

Qliphoth

Qliphoth is the Plural form of *qlipha*, 'shell', or 'husk'. The Qliphoth are the unbalanced forces of the universe, composed of 'units' (or fragments) that are by themselves incomplete and therefore require temporary union with other forces to find stability. Such stability is naturally relative to other things, and temporary; and so instability is really the defining term here. The Qliphoth form the great dragon called Leviathan in the Bible, and whose name derives from the Hebrew word LVH meaning 'to join, lend, borrow'.

There is thus direct comparison between the Qliphoth and vampirical entities, for redemption comes about only through union with the divine or eternal. The realm of the Qliphoth is the lunar or astral underworld of shadows, elemental spirits, man's natural soul and the shells of the dead—the underworld or 'fallen' aspect of the Scarlet Woman. In the Qabalah this material world is referred to as Assiah, which is cut off from the rest of the Tree of Life by the fall through which it has been divided from spirit.

The doctrine of the Qliphoth is closely related to that of the Egyptian Ka and Khaibet. The force sustaining the life of the Qliphoth is the power of Hadit transmitted to the human soul by the Beast or power hidden within nature. In the fallen universe, where man has freewill, this power is able to operate independently from the True Will. The forms that are ensouled as a result of man's unregenerate desire body are illusory, mutable, perishable and vampirical. They imprison and obsess the soul who sustains them, and drain away all her energy, eventually leading her to hell and dispersion in the underworld. To be free from enslavement to the Qliphoth, the Initiate must master, release and transmute the life force they entrap. The Great Work is thus primarily that of transmutation of the Qliphoth; the unbalanced forces of the natural soul must be organised through union with the word of the True Will. Traditional doctrines provide means for this, such as rites, observances, yoga and even social ordering in such as has survived in truly traditional civilisations. In the post-industrial and technological age, all such means have been rejected and only the counterfeit forms encouraged or permitted. Thus the very nature of 'modern life' involves slavery to vampiric, Qliphotic forces.

—See also: Beast; Fall; Hadit; Ka; Khu; Scarlet Woman.

Ra

Ra is ostensibly the Egyptian sun god, but is much more than that, and was never intended to symbolise the visible Sun, as is by now frequently supposed by profane scholars. Ra is, in his most supreme aspect, identical to the Hindu Brahma Nirguna, 'without attributes'. Indeed, the Hindus use identical solar symbolism to represent the Brahma that cannot otherwise be symbolised.

In ontological and cosmological terms (these not being in any way separate), Ra is 'self-created', and emerges from the primordial Nun in the form of Khephra, the sacred beetle. Ra travels the indefinite reach of the heavens in his 'boat of a million years'. While this is most always associated by commentators with periodic daily and annual cycles, one of Ra's secrets is that he ordains magnitudinous Cosmic Cycles. The term 'million years' simply means 'uncountable'; it was never intended to be an exact quantity.

—See also: Khabs; Khephra; Khu; Nun.

Ra Hoor Khuit

Ra Hoor Khuit is the Egyptian god of Force and Fire, that is, of manifestation, at least in the most outward sense. He is the projected aspect of the double god Heru-ra-ha, born of the interaction of Nuit and Hadit—or circle rotating about the point, if we use geometric symbolism. His complement is Hoor-paar-kraat, the unmanifest or 'hidden universe'. If we regard these two as sacerdotal authority and temporal power, as exemplifed by the priesthood and warrior caste, then the silent twin is really the superior—or should be in a properly organised civilisation. Ra Hoor Khuit projects the True Will going forth from Nuit and Hadit into creation or nature. He is a form of the god Hrumachis, the 'god of the two horizons', which refers to the symbol of the sun between sunrise and sunset as dual means of manifestation and life, and of which the further and most complete symbol is the Sphinx.

—See also: Hadit; Heru-ra-ha; Hoor-paar-kraat; Horus; Hrumachis; Nuit; Sphinx.

Ruach

The Ruach is one of the five parts of the human soul in the Qabalah. On the Tree of Life, the Ruach comprises the seven sephiroth from Chesed to Yesod, the latter being its point of contact with the part of the soul called Nephesch.

Ruach is the Hebrew word for 'breath, scent or fragrance'. The word Ruach is used for 'spirit', the breath of life forming and animating the universe. In the book of Genesis, I: 2, this spirit is described as the primal force emerging from chaos:

> And the earth was without form, and void; and darkness was upon the face of the deep. And the spirit of God moved upon the face of the waters.

The Ruach radiates out of the centre of consciousness called Khabs in Liber AL vel Legis, and permeates all worlds of manifestation.

—See also: Khabs; Nephesch; Soul.

Scarlet Woman

The name 'Scarlet Woman' is derived from St. John's book of Revelation, in which it is given to the prostitute Babylon (Revelation 17: 17–18). Together with the 'Beast', she represents the force ruling the material universe, which is vampiric or Qliphotic. The name Babylon derives from 'Babel', meaning 'anointed' as well as 'mix, mingle and confuse' in Hebrew. In earlier languages it means simply the 'Gates of the City', typified by Ishtar and her two lions guarding the city of Babylon.

As manifested existence and life, the Scarlet Woman is multiplicity, the production of Maya in the Hindu doctrines. Her name is also related to the ancient Egyptian word for the soul, Ba. Her sacrament is bread, the visible manifestation of the spirit (as host), and the preserver of life. Bread, having many grains in one whole substance, represents multiplicity. Bread and cakes (see Liber AL, III: 25) are the traditional sacrament of the goddess in most, if not all of her aspects.

Revelation tells the allegorical story of the initiatory death of the Scarlet Woman, through which she is taken as bride by the Lamb and transfigured into the heavenly Jerusalem—or renewal of the Word at the spring equinox of Aries—see Revelation 21. The nuptial feast that follows the hour of doom of the Scarlet Woman is a celebration of the soul's victory over death and world illusion, and of her union with the eternal.

The name of the Scarlet Woman is spelled *Babalon* in Elizabethan alchemist John Dee's Enochian Calls. The name Qabalistically adds to 156, which is the product of 13 x 12, the 'unity of the Zodiac'. The Zodiac is the belt or girdle of the goddess in all ancient traditions.

Liber AL vel Legis reveals that Hadit, the giver of life, manifests Nuit as the Scarlet Woman, the supernal Khu and the archetypal world of Briah. In manifesting her, he manifests life, the body or matrix in which he comes into existence as the Beast, the supernal Khabs and world of Atziluth. In the Scarlet Woman 'is all power given' (Liber AL, I: 15). The power is that of the Serpent of Knowledge animating the life of the Scarlet Woman and secretly radiating from the Khabs contained within her.

Above the Abyss, the Scarlet Woman is the body of Nuit, the company of heaven, the intelligence referred to as Neschemah in the Qabalah. In her underworld aspect the Scarlet Woman is manifested as the great dragon, the material and visible world (Assiah) at the base of the Tree. Therein dwell man, demons, and the Qliphoth or shells of the dead. The descent of Babalon or the Scarlet Woman into the underworld was originally not seen as a 'fall from grace', but as a heroic act. By so doing, she is able to awaken the power of the Beast for the purposes of initiation.

So far as the 'sinful' nature of the Scarlet Woman is concerned, it is curious to note that in Hebrew the word 'sin' actually means 'thorn' and 'clay'. Thorny plants such as the acacia or rose symbolise the horns of the crescent moon. The moon itself, like the clay shaped by the hands of the divine potter Ptah, is a symbol of the body and the natural soul. Liber AL vel Legis, I: 16, describes the Scarlet Woman as being 'a moon'; as a moon, she is containment and receptivity, as well as the division into parts of cyclical, phasic existence. She is the placenta feeding the magical embryo or Khabs.

—See also: Beast; Briah; Khabs; Khu; Nephesch; Neschemah; Soul; Qliphoth.

Set

Set was the primordial god of the Egyptians, whose name has the meaning, 'black', also 'foundation'—a name that points to the very origins of the primordial tradition in the present cycle of humanity. Set is the son of the great mother goddess Nuit-Typhon-Draco. He also embodies the principles of dividing, cleaving, breaking, slaying and reversing. Set is the 'slayer of the real' who breaks the circle of the 'infinite' to produce the worlds of manifestation. Conversely, Set moves through creation as the destroyer or transformer, perpetually annihilating the forms he created out of chaos or the undifferentiated ground.

Set's natural abode or dwelling place is the desert, the burning and transforming expanse of the Abyss in which knowledge and all the contents of mind turn to dust. Set is always where consciousness, embodied by his twin brother Horus, is *not*. Through polarisation, Set both restores equilibrium by destroying whatever is excess, and creating movement where there is inertia. He is the opposer and the accuser or Adversary, the dark sun who presides over all that is opposite and 'outside'—all that is other, unseen and unexpected.

Set is the 'sun of midnight' who is 'ever a son' (Liber AL, III: 74). He is the beginning and the end, the Alpha and the Omega. As such he is the Lord of Initiation eternally moving consciousness beyond defined boundaries, whether towards or away from manifestation. Together, Set and Horus, the sky by night and the sky by day, form a ladder between heaven and earth.

As the appointer of life and death, Set is the Lord of Hell or Amenta. Evoker of the *nigredo*, he presides over the alchemical dross, the transmutation of which is the secret of the Great Work. The Setian forces of dispersion and change are the power enabling the cyclical renewal of the physical universe as well as its dissolution at the end of time.

Set is closely associated with Hadit and his manifestation, the Beast. The polarity of Set and Horus was known at Aunnu (Heliopolis) as the double god Heru-Set, whose attributes are similar to those of Heru-ra-ha. Aunnu was considered to be the birthplace of Horus, the Word.

—See also: Heru-ra-ha; Hoor-paar-kraat; Horus; Ra Hoor Khuit.

Sirius

Sirius was known to the Egyptians as Sothis, meaning 'Soul of Isis' in Greek, and also known as the Dog Star, as it follows the great constellation of Orion, known as the Hunter or Long-strider. Sirius is sometimes referred to as sun-behind-the sun, the principial source of the solar system, the renewer of time-cycles. Sirius is the star of Set, whose mother is Hathoor, called Ahathoor in Liber AL.

In ancient Egypt, Sirius was called the 'Opener of the Year' as her rising corresponds to the rising of the Nile, the river whose waters once brought life to the land and announced the renewal of the seasonal cycle.

—See also: Ahathoor; Set.

Soul

The Hebrew word for 'soul' is Nephesch, meaning literally 'to take breath'. In the biblical book of Genesis, II: 7, the creation of the soul by the demiurge is described as follows:

> And the Lord God formed man of the dust of the ground, and breathed into his nostrils the breath of life; and man became a living soul.

The life-giving breath taken in by the soul is called the Ruach, a Hebrew word that means breath but also smell, scent or fragrance. The soul may thus be defined as substance animated by the divine breath or Word. In classical Greek, the soul is called Psyche that, like the Hebrew Nephesch, means the 'breath of life'. The Greeks used the word Psyche to generally refer to everything in which there is life. They regarded the soul as the vital force that animates the body and shows itself in breathing. The full meaning of the word Psyche thus covered the dual principles of name and form, the life-giving power of the divine breath or Ruach and the living creature or Nephesch it animates.

In biblical writings, the Nephesch is sometimes simply referred to as 'the flesh'. In Liber AL vel Legis, life and the life-giving power of the divine breath or Word are associated with Hadit, who declares that he is 'Life and the giver of Life' (II: 6). Hadit is the power hidden behind the life of the soul, whom he manifests as the Scarlet Woman. His life-giving power is manifested as the Beast.

Liber AL vel Legis also uses two Egyptian terms to refer to the matrix of life who takes in the divine breath and the source of this breath. These are called the Khu and the Khabs. Owing to the division of consciousness or 'fall', these twin principles are themselves doubled. The Khabs and the Khu each dwell at once in heaven, the realm of supra-human states of being, where they are celestial and in perfect union, and in time, where they are mortal humans and separate from each other. The natural soul, called Ka by the ancient Egyptians, is granted freewill. Her life is individual and personal. She is the seat of the mind, will, appetites, desires and passions.

The life of the fallen soul is in nature, and is consequently mortal, mutable and perishable. To achieve Hadit, the natural soul must be reunited with her counterpart that dwells in the immutable realm of spirit. There, her substance is transmuted; no longer bound to that which perishes, she becomes one with the word of her True Will.

In the Qabalah, the soul of man is represented as having five parts: the Yechidah, Chiah, Neschemah, Ruach and Nephesch.

—See also: Beast; Chiah; Fall; Hadit; Yechidah; Khabs; Khu; Nephesch; Neschemah; Ruach; Scarlet Woman.

Sphinx

The Sphinx, as physical object, is the ancient Egyptian stone figure situated on the plateau of Giza near the Pyramids. The Sphinx has a human face and lion's body, representing sacerdotal authority (the priesthood) and temporal power (the nobles and warriors). The man and the lion are symbols of the astrological signs of Aquarius and Leo, the Star and the Snake of Liber AL. These are the attributes of Nuit and Hadit, and of their manifestation, the Beast and Scarlet Woman, or the Khabs and the Khu.

The mystery of the Sphinx is that of the divine, immutable principle and the mutable, cyclical nature of the life of the universe and the human soul. This passes through four stages: The Golden Age, where man is closest to spiritual reality. The Silver Age, where is the first admixture of necessity and adaptive means but for the most part truth prevails. The Bronze Age, of which it could be said that 'good' and 'evil' come about in the world. Finally, the Age of Iron or Kali Yuga, where oral traditions are written down and need for initiation arises. The use of magick comes about and sometimes it becomes 'black magic', when the supreme principle is either knowingly denied or simply absent by ignorance. Towards the end of the Kali Yuga man loses sight of all spiritual reality and constructs counterfeits of initiation, such as psychological analysis. Finally there is death and dissolution of this world at the end of time. The return to eternity comes about in an 'instant', as does the Golden Age of a new Cosmic Cycle—but there is no return to the previous state.

In classical symbolism, the Sphinx is sometimes represented as a fourfold creature bearing the attributes of all four cardinal points. With a human face, the body of a bull, the feet of a lion and the wings of an eagle, this form of the Sphinx was developed from the original image of the dual Egyptian Sphinx. The word 'sphinx' itself comes from the Greek *sphingein*, a word that means 'to draw tight', in other words, to bring to unity. One of the images of this metamorphic cycle of life, with its four cardinal points, is the circle of the Zodiac, symbol of the celestial Khu.

The Sphinx stands at the heart of its twelve signs, of which four are fixed: Leo, Aquarius, Taurus and Scorpio, the four aspects of the Sphinx. The number 12 lies at the basis of the ancient Egyptian description of the great life cycle of the universe, the macrocosm, and of its microcosmic counterpart, the human soul. The macrocosmic cycle was referred to by the Greeks and Persians as the Great Year, one half of a full precession of the equinoxes through which the earth's pole travels across twelve 'months', the twelve astrological ages that together extend over a period of approximately 26,000 years.

The microcosmic cycle of the soul is described as having twelve hours, the sixth hour being the halfway mark at which the soul begins her descent in the underworld. The ninth hour is that of the transmutation of the elements of the physical body, which is followed by the hour of judgement. It then takes three more hours for the justified soul to rise from death and fully resurrect—hence the use of identical symbolism throughout the Gospel narrative of the life and death of Christ Jesus.

The date at which the Egyptian Sphinx was built is speculative, but the constellation of Leo the Lion was rising in the direction which the Sphinx is facing around 10,000 BC. At this time, the Sphinx—or its predecessor—would have been perfectly aligned with the polarity formed by Leo and Aquarius, or Hadit and Nuit. Taking the starting point for the Sphinx from that 'First Time', as it was referred to by the ancient Egyptians, the astrological Age of Aquarius of the present time represents the 6th hour of night, the beginning of the full descent of the soul into the underworld and in material terms, the end of time and great dissolution of the world (Sanskrit *mahapralaya*).

Horus is also the god of the Sphinx, his many forms corresponding to the various stages of transformation through which passes the life of the universe, and of the soul also. The name Horus is closely related to the Greek word *hora*, meaning 'season, hour', the very principles of division into time.

—See also: Ankh-af-na-khonsu; Beast; Fall; Hadit; Horus; Khabs; Khu; Scarlet Woman.

Spirit

Spirit is, properly speaking, the Absolute, Infinite and Everlasting. The same word is used, with a downwardly transposed meaning, as the breath, intelligence or fragrance transmitting the Word to all of creation or the manifest worlds.

According to Liber AL vel Legis, the source of this intelligence is Hadit. The transmitter is the Beast; the creation it animates is the Scarlet Woman or soul. As a centre of consciousness by which spirit may be realised, the Beast is a Khabs, Star, or Holy Guardian Angel. As a body permeated by spirit, the Scarlet Woman is the Khu, and the human soul.

—See also: Beast; Hadit; Khabs; Khu; Scarlet Woman; Soul.

Star

The star or Khabs is the true nature and 'centre' of every man and every woman, as revealed by Nuit in Liber AL, I: 3.

—See also: Khabs.

Stele of Revealing

The *Stele of Revealing* is a title given to the funeral stone of a XXVIth dynasty Egyptian priest of the cult of Ankh-af-na-khonsu, who lived around the year 600 BC. While a priest at Thebes, Ankh-af-na-khonsu received the revelation that is recorded on his funeral stone. This stele was exhibited at the Cairo museum at the time when Aleister and Rose Crowley were honeymooning in Egypt in 1904. Its exhibit number was 666, the number of the Beast of St. John's book of Revelation. Liber AL vel Legis refers to the stele as 'the Abomination of Desolation', a term borrowed from the Old Testament where it appears in Daniel's prophesy on the 'end of time' (Daniel, 12). Christ Jesus quoted the term later in the eschatological discourses recorded in the Gospels of St Matthew and Mark (Matthew, 24: 15, Mark, 13: 14).

—See also: Abyss; Ankh-af-na-khonsu; Beast; Heaven, company of.

Tetragrammaton

In classical Qabalah, Tetragrammaton refers to the four letters of the Hebrew name of God: Yod, Hé, Vav, Hé (IHVH, Yahweh or Jehovah). The Yod corresponds to the principial world, Atziluth, referred to as Father in the formula of Tetragrammaton. The first Hé corresponds to the archetypal world, Briah, referred to as the Mother. The Vav corresponds to the formative world, Yetzirah, referred to as the Son. The Hé final corresponds to the material world, Assiah, referred to as the Daughter. The four principles embody, among other things, the cardinal points of the cycle of consciousness and life of the soul through creation, fall, death and redemption. The numerical formula of the letters corresponds to the Pythagorean Tetractys:

$$1 + 2 + 3 + 4 = 10$$

The name itself (IHVH) adds to 26, which is the number of the pyramid (10) surmounting the cube (16)—thus a complete numerical cosmograph. The Qabalistic formula of Tetragrammaton teaches that the fallen soul, the daughter (Hé-final), is to marry the son (Vav), the Holy Guardian Angel, to be placed back on the throne of her mother (first Hé) and reunited with her father (Yod), the principle.

The four Hebrew letters corresponding to the *elements* are often used in contemporary Hermetic or theurgical operations, as the biblical demiurge is incompatible with all other gods. The Hermetic name of Tetragrammaton is thus Shematah (ShMATh): Shin (Atziluth), Mem (Briah), Aleph (Yetzirah) and Tav (Assiah). Shematah means 'The Name', and is the word of IAO, as the Beginning and the End (ATh). Shematah is the immortal essence realised in the substance of flesh, and the perfected word of Ma'at.

In Liber AL vel Legis, the four principles are seen to rest on the doubling of one original polarity, the Beast and the Scarlet Woman, or the Khabs and the Khu. The doubling comes about through descent into the underworld, as a necessary preparation for ascent, or re-ascent (in the case of an avatar).

On their emergence, the Khabs and Khu correspond to Logos (Shin) and Matrix (Mem) of Tetragrammaton. Above the Abyss, the twin principles are in perfect union. Below the Abyss or in the underworld, the Khabs and Khu are the Holy Guardian Angel (Aleph) and the natural soul (Tav). Through the division of consciousness 'for the chance of union' that is symbolised by the letter Zain, the two are in a state of separation, and are confounded by Eros and Thanatos. The Law of Thelema, 'love under will', is the means of their reunion. Seen in this way, the formula of Tetragrammaton expresses the mystery of the Sphinx.

—See also: Assiah; Atziluth; Beast; Briah; Fall; Holy Guardian Angel; Khabs; Khu; Scarlet Woman; Sphinx; Thelema; Worlds, Four; Yetzirah; Zain.

Thebes

The nature of the work that was performed by Initiates in Thebes is worth noting, as it sheds much light on some of the more obscure passages of the (Egyptian) Book of the Law. A group of temples at Thebes (Karnak) consecrated to the Theban Triad, Amoun, Mut and Khonsu, is called Apet-Sut. The word *sut* means place, and is also a root of the name Set.

The word *apet*, designating the type of the female hippopotamus whose enormous belly symbolises the gestating womb, is derived from the root *ip*, meaning 'to count', 'to enumerate'. Apet-Sut can thus be translated as 'Enumerator of the Places', for the name implies that gestation is identified with counting. Numbers are thus seen as generative powers.

While Heliopolis and Memphis paid tribute to an Ennead of nine Neteru or gods, and Hermopolis to an Ogdoad of eight, Karnak replaced this with an unusual fifteen Neteru. Fifteen is a number of the primordial goddess and her divine child, Set-Typhon. More specifically, fifteen is descriptive of her *kalas* or emanations, which count the cyclical motion of the breath (*prana*) of life.

At Thebes, the Hidden God known there by the name of Amoun is represented by a walking figure, the vital breath that lives in all things and that moves by numbers.[153] Each one of the temples of Apet-Sut is consecrated to a particular Neter, which is a principle or mode of action of the Hidden God.[154] The numbers conceal—and reveal—the Neteru. Thebes is therefore the centre of instruction concerned with the science of numbers par excellence. It is also the centre concerned with the precession of the equinoxes, and the 'enumeration of the place' of Ra, as symbolised by the light of the Sun passing around the Zodiac belt.

The two principal deities of the Theban Triad, Amoun and Mut, whose child is Khonsu, correspond astrologically to the signs of Aries and Libra—Amoun is often depicted as ram-headed, while Mut is associated with Ma'at and her scales. Aries and Libra are the two signs entered by the sun at the equinoxes. Khonsu carries the Eye of Ra, showing that, as the child of Amoun and Mut, he is the child of the enumeration of the cycle of the sun.

---

[153] The vital breath 'moves by numbers' since it is periodical, cyclical, and rhythmical—its movement has a count. Such is the basis of the numerical aspect of the Qabalah where numbers are living entities, and of the science of numbers in all traditions.

[154] The Hidden God was known at Thebes as Amoun, 'The Concealed' or 'Hidden Countenance'. Amoun is hidden or concealed because he is invisible, below the horizon where the sun sets and where, in Egyptian symbolism, the sun god Ra enters the body of Nuit. The horizon is that which divides waking or day-time consciousness from dreaming or night-time consciousness. The Hidden God is a term interchangeable with that of the Holy Guardian Angel—though this should not be confused with mere dream or imagining.

It is therefore from Thebes that the precession of the equinoxes is declared. This is identical with the utterance of the Word that must become flesh. The Word made flesh is at the heart of the esoteric doctrine of ancient Egypt, and therefore of Liber AL vel Legis.

—See also: Ankh-af-na-khonsu; Initiation, Egyptian, centres of; Ma'at.

Thebes—warrior lord of

The warrior lord of Thebes refers to both a Theban high priest of the cult of Ankh-af-na-khonsu, and the form of Horus worshipped at Thebes as Mentu.

—See also: Ankh-af-na-khonsu; Mentu; Thebes.

Thelema

Θελημα is the Greek word for 'will', and is the word of the law given by Nuit in chapter one of Liber AL vel Legis. By Greek Qabalah, the number of Thelema is 93. Thelema is therefore identical to Agape (Αγαπη), spiritual or impersonal love, which also has the value of 93. In the New Testament, the word Thelema occurs very frequently (in Greek) and nearly always refers to the will of God, not that of man. The Greek word Agape also occurs frequently, and is usually translated as 'charity', which, in the etymological and original sense, has nothing to do with the modern notion of the word, and is linked to *charisma*, 'divine grace'. This grace and charisma is also obfuscated in meaning by modern (profane) convention. It is in fact a spiritual influence.

See Aeon; Horus; Nuit.

Thoth (or Tahuti)

Thoth is the Egyptian god of writing and magick; the utterer of the Word, the intelligence of God and male counterpart of Ma'at. He is also, and most particularly, the conveyor of the primordial tradition and its sacerdotal authority. Thoth was known to the Greeks as Hermes, and to the Romans as Mercury. The ancient Egyptians attributed the god Set to the planet Mercury, while originally Thoth was associated with the Moon as the marker of time. This points to the close relationship between Set and Thoth. Thoth gradually assimilated the attributes of Set as the latter became demonised over the course of the Kali Yuga or Age of Iron.

—See also: Ma'at; Set.

Tum

Tum was the first fully anthropomorphic god representing Ra as the sun in the East. Later, his position moved to the West and he came to represent the setting of Ra in the underworld—the reflection of Nuit's body. Tum thus became the god below the horizon, identical to Amoun the 'Hidden God', as known at Thebes. At Aunnu, Tum was Ra-Hoor when rising in the East, Ra-Tum when setting in the West, and the double head of the boat of Ra, also sometimes represented with Ma'at and Thoth directing its course. His earliest, primal form was that of Bes, the dwarf-self.

—See also: Aunnu; Holy Guardian Angel; Ra; Thebes.

Typhon

Typhon is the Greek name for the multi-faceted god who perpetually destroys forms to bring about change in the universe. He appears under many names and forms, including Hadit, Set, Bes, or 'the Beast'. One of his symbols is the Egyptian Sphinx. Typhon is the son who manifests his mother, the primal goddess who through him takes on any number of aspects. The constellation named by the Egyptians as the 'Thigh' (Ursa Major) was her stellar symbol. The association between the constellation of Ursa Major and the star at the North Pole is astronomically as well as esoterically significant.

See also: Beast; Hadit; Nuit; Set; Sphinx.

Worlds, Four

The Four Worlds of the Qabalah are, starting from the supernals: Atziluth, the principial world; Briah, the archetypal world; Yetzirah, the formative world; Assiah, the material world. The mystery of the interaction of these four worlds is summed up in the Qabalistic formula of Tetragrammaton.

—See also: Assiah, Atziluth, Briah, Tetragrammaton and Yetzirah.

Yechidah

In the Qabalah, the Yechidah refers to one of the five parts of the human soul, of which it is the quintessence. On the Tree of Life, the Yechidah is attributed to the sphere of Kether in the microcosm. The Hebrew word Yechidah has the meaning, 'one, only; only child'. It refers to the only begotten child of the great mother goddess Nuit: Hadit or Set, the divine Word. The title of 'only begotten son' is also given to Christ Jesus in the Gospels, such as in John I: 18 where John the Baptist says:

> No man hath seen God at any time; the only begotten son, which is in the bosom of the father, he hath declared him.

The word Yechidah derives from *yechid*, meaning 'united, joined', indicative of the inseparable nature of the son and the mother-father god. That is, of Hadit and Nuit, or the Sphinx. In the Hindu tradition, the Yechidah is called Atma, who is considered to be inseparable in reality from the absolute (or impersonal) Brahma.

Yetzirah

Yetzirah is the Hebrew word for 'formation' and is the name of the formative world in the Qabalah. Yetzirah corresponds to the seven sephiroth from Chesed to Yesod, that is, to the part of the soul called Ruach. Yetzirah also corresponds to the letter Vav of the formula of Tetragrammaton. The intelligence ruling over Yetzirah is the Beast or Khabs. By Hebrew Qabalah, the number of Yetzirah is 305. This is also the number of 'a curving, bending', pointing to the relationship between the formative world of Yetzirah and the curvature of time and space that underlies the Cosmic Cycles governing the material world, Assiah.

The number 305 also corresponds to the Hebrew word for 'Lamb', relating Yetzirah to the 'Lamb of God', one of the titles given to Christ Jesus in the Gospel of St. John. The 'Christ' or 'anointed one' is the Holy Guardian Angel, the life-giving spirit.

Further numeric correspondences to Yetzirah are the Hebrew word for 'dazzling with light', and the closing phrase of the twelfth chapter of the book of Daniel, 'the end of days'. It is in this chapter of Daniel that appears the first biblical reference to the 'Abomination of Desolation', a name given to the *Stele of Revealing* in Liber AL vel Legis. Yetzirah is the world which the soul must pass through to reach the end of time, cross the Abyss and enter eternity.

—See also Abyss; Beast; Heaven, Company of; Khabs; Ruach; Stele of Revealing; Tetragrammaton; Worlds, Four.

Zain (or Zayin)

Zain is the name of the Hebrew letter corresponding to the number seven and the Hebrew word for 'sword' (ז). The sword is a symbol of the divine Word cutting through the analogous circle of 'infinity' to produce manifest existence. The existence of such creation depends on the dualistic nature of the human mind. The principle embodied by the sword is division and therefore doubling—a principle also associated with the Egyptian god Set.

The name of Set is related to the word Sept, meaning 'seven'. The correspondences to Zain are manifold. Beginning with the traditional Qabalistic attributions, Zain is the path of the Tree of Life that links Tiphereth to Binah. The corresponding Tarot Atu is the Lovers VI, the twins representing all opposites, which are, at a further stage, realised as complementary as all dualities are transcended by the principle that unites them.

The path of Zain is attributed to the astrological sign of Gemini, itself ruled by the god Mercury. Mercury is the Roman equivalent of the Egyptian god Thoth, the utterer of the divine Word and the male counterpart of Ma'at, goddess of justice, truth and balance. Through the Age of Kali Yuga the god Set, who was identified with Mercury, became increasingly demonised in Egypt; his positive attributes were gradually transferred to Thoth, whose totem animal is the Ibis. Thoth is the male counterpart of Ma'at. Together, Thoth and Ma'at oversee the transmission of the divine Word or True Will. Zain, the path by which the Word begets duality across the Abyss, and Lamed, the Ma'atian path through which duality is maintained in equilibrium below the Abyss, are therefore complementary.

—See also: Abyss; Ma'at; Set.

Selected Works of Oliver St. John

Hermetic Astrology (2015)
Magical Theurgy—Rituals of the Tarot (2015)
The Enterer of the Threshold (2016)
Liber 373 Astrum Draconis (2017)
Hermetic Qabalah Foundation—Complete Course (2018)
Babalon Unveiled! Thelemic Monographs (2019)
Ritual Magick—Initiation of the Star and Snake (2019)
Nu Hermetica—Initiation and Metaphysical Reality (2021)
The Way of Knowledge in the Reign of Antichrist (2022)
Thirty-two paths of Wisdom (2023)
Thunder Perfect Gnosis—Intellectual Flower of Mind (2023)
Metamorphosis—Hermetic Science and Yoga Power (2024)
Advaita Vedanta—Question of the Real (2025)
Egyptian Tarot and Tarot Cards (2025)

(The dates given are the first publication date. Most of these books have been revised in new editions since then. We recommend that our students read the most recent editions of these books, which can be found easily on our website, given below.)

Contact the O∴A∴

Contact details and information is posted on our website:

www.ordoastri.org

www.ingramcontent.com/pod-product-compliance
Lightning Source LLC
Chambersburg PA
CBHW050835160426
43192CB00010B/2033